Jeb Jackson was the enemy.

At least, Megan MacKay had thought so ever since her father had disappeared after a midnight poker game with Jeb, and Jeb had produced the crumpled deed to her father's ranch along with that cryptic promissory note, which read, "If I lose this hand, my ranch goes to Jeb…if he'll swear to take care of my daughter, Megan, as part of the bargain. Glen MacKay."

Jeb had sworn readily enough to take care of the redheaded minx he'd loved as his kid sister, never thinking she'd see his winning her ranch as the ultimate betrayal. Never thinking that, in the years that would pass, taking care of Megan would be a whole lot harder than running the ranch.

Suddenly, just as Jeb has reached his wits' end with the reckless pranks of this feisty she-devil, he discovers that he wants to possess her a whole lot more than he wants her ranch. The stakes are now higher than those in that first poker game, for Jeb must risk his heart to win her soul.

Please address questions and book requests to: Silhouette Reader Service
U.S.: 5010 Walden Ave., P.O. Box 1325, Buffalo, NY 14269
Canadian: P.O. Box 609, Fort Erie, Ont. L2A 5X3

48

WESTERN *Lovers*™

ANN MAJOR

DESTINY'S CHILD

Silhouette Books

Published by Silhouette Books
America's Publisher of Contemporary Romance

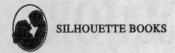 **SILHOUETTE BOOKS**

ISBN 0-373-30196-0

DESTINY'S CHILD

Copyright © 1988 by Ann Major

All rights reserved. Except for use in any review, the reproduction
or utilization of this work in whole or in part in any form by any
electronic, mechanical or other means, now known or hereafter
invented, including xerography, photocopying and recording, or in
any information storage or retrieval system, is forbidden without
the written permission of the editorial office, Silhouette Books,
300 East 42nd Street, New York, NY 10017 U.S.A.

All characters in this book have no existence outside the imagination of
the author and have no relation whatsoever to anyone bearing the same
name or names. They are not even distantly inspired by any individual
known or unknown to the author, and all incidents are pure invention.

This edition published by arrangement with Harlequin Books S.A.

® and TM are trademarks of Harlequin Books S.A., used under license.
Trademarks indicated with ® are registered in the United States Patent
and Trademark Office, the Canadian Trade Marks Office and in other
countries.

Visit Silhouette at www.eHarlequin.com

Printed in U.S.A.

This book is dedicated to my dearest friend—
Diana Gafford—for being one of the most beautiful people
I've ever known.

One

It was a wild, moonless night with a bank of low clouds hiding the stars—the kind of south Texas spring night when the darkness itself seems alive. A man could get tired just being out in it. Every branch in the dense oak motts and mesquite thickets twisted and groaned. Every blade of thin, brown bluestem lashed at Caesar's hooves as he picked his way wearily across the sandy pastures. The heat of the day lingered in that billowing wind—thick, humid, inescapable.

Jeb Jackson had been slumped in his saddle since dawn inspecting some of the more remote parts of his ranch, which he couldn't reach in his four-wheel drive because the pastures were choked by ebony, shin oak, granjeno and huisache. Usually Jeb left the brute work of scouring these deep and thorny thickets to his vaqueros, but there were times when he gave in to a certain edginess in his nature and took a day away from the office, the telephone and the board of directors to personally inspect his windmills, fences and cattle. Jackson Ranch was a hands-on operation, and everybody knew that Jeb Jackson would never ask a man, woman or child to do something he wasn't ready to do himself. Because he ran his empire with an iron hand, his Mexican-American vaqueros called him *El Rey*, the king. When Jeb gave orders, he expected instant obedience, and he got it.

With one exception.

Why Jeb was so lenient with his beautiful, rebellious pilot, Megan MacKay, nobody knew.

There was a rumor among the men that Jeb had won her daddy Glen MacKay's ranch in a poker game—and that Glen's daughter had been part of the package, that one night Jeb had had her, and she'd hated him ever since.

But the women said knowingly that the last part of the story couldn't be true. They thought any girl lucky enough to have Jeb Jackson for a night wouldn't hate him half as much as Megan did. He'd always had a way with women. It was his incredible smile, some said, but there were also those who whispered slyly that it was much, much more than his smile.

He was tall and dark, with a sleek, muscled body that was as dangerous and graceful as a tiger's. His bold, black eyes slanted sensually beneath heavy dark brows. His hair was black and worn carelessly long, falling across his tanned brow, curling against the top of his collar. He had a reputation for toughness, an instinct for getting his way and a fierce sense of duty to his family.

There had been rumors about Jeb and Megan for years, but there was no way of knowing the truth. Glen MacKay had run off for good. His son Kirk wasn't talking. Nobody dared to ask Megan or Jeb.

When Jeb married Emmy Spencer, the rumors simmered down for a while. Then Emmy died. Megan came home from college and flight school, and the sparks began to fly between the king and the pilot. Many recalled the old story and continued to wonder.

Jeb felt bone-weary from the long day. Every muscle in his body ached. Not that he hadn't been bred to hard work and long hours—he had. Ranching in arid south Texas was a tough business; ranchers had to be tough men.

Jeb didn't mind the hard outdoor work as much as he minded the endless worrying over money. The Jacksons were land-rich and cash-poor. Drought, disease, taxes, a myriad of new paralyzing government regulations and low cattle and oil prices had forced Jeb to borrow heavily to meet the ranch's obligations. If the situation didn't change drastically, and soon, he would be forced to start selling the ranch's assets one by one. Today Jeb had been down to the MacKay land to meet with Jack Robards, the oilman who was interested in taking a lease on some acreage.

The wind howled through an oak mott, rustling the leaves and the grasses. Caesar whinnied as a cactus thorn bit into his leg.

"Easy, boy," Jeb whispered. He pulled his bandanna up over his nose and mouth so he could breathe without taking in gulps of dust. "We're almost home." He pulled his Stetson lower on his forehead, but there was little he could do to protect his red-rimmed eyes as he peered through the grit for some sign of the Big House.

Jeb was ready to hand Caesar over to Mario and enjoy the comfort of a hot shower and a warm supper. Then he would call his girlfriend, Janelle Jacobs, who lived in California.

Most of all, he wanted to collapse into his bed.

The wind would probably die down around dawn and then come up again before noon. Tomorrow would be another humid, white day. Jeb hated these smothering white days. They always put him on edge and made the muscles at the back of his skull tight. He had a headache from fighting the wind and the range and the animals.

Suddenly, from out of nowhere, there came a storm of sound in the swirling, humid darkness.

Caesar screamed and reared exactly as he had the time he almost stepped in a nest of sidewinders.

Jeb cursed under his breath, dug his knees into Caesar's flanks and jerked hard on the reins. When the quarter horse quieted, Jeb sat rigidly upright in his saddle, straining to listen.

From above the cloak of clouds throbbed the unmistakable motor of a single, fragile engine.

It flew over and was gone.

It was a plane, flying low in the clouds. There was something secretive, something illicit about the sound, and Jeb felt an uneasy sensation in the middle of his gut.

Most south Texas ranchers in the same circumstances would have imagined a drug runner flying in from Mexico.

Jeb thought of Megan MacKay. Her brother Kirk had disappeared two days before on one of his mysterious missions.

Jeb quashed the thought and tried to reassure himself. "Hell, it was only a drug runner. Had to be. Perfect night for it."

Kirk had promised he would be back by noon today.

Megan was wild, but she wasn't crazy. She would never go up on a night like this.

What if she'd found out Kirk was in trouble?

Jeb felt the familiar tightening in his gut again. Only Megan could make his insides knot up like this.

His hands clenched around the reins, and he dug his heels into Caesar.

Megan MacKay would do anything.

Damn! If that was Megan up there, risking her neck and his plane, he'd fire her this time, once and for all.

To hell with the promise he'd made Glen MacKay ten years ago! Jeb didn't like being pushed, and that redheaded she-devil had pushed him about as far as any man could be pushed.

Two

Horseshoes rang on concrete as Jeb rode into the stable. Funny how the weariness always went out of Caesar's step the closer he got to his stall and a fresh bale of hay. Jeb dismounted and slapped the reins into the callused brown palm of his stable boy.

"Is MacKay back?" Jeb demanded.

Mario shook his dark head and lowered his eyes. Nobody liked giving the boss bad news. Jeb towered over the thin vaquero and regarded him sharply. The two spoke rapidly in Spanish, the second language of the ranch, and as they did, Jeb's frown deepened.

Without a word Jeb strode toward Kirk's office and pushed the door open. A window unit gushed ice-cold air. Jeb flipped on the light switch, blinked hard and stared into the fluorescent glare. The insides of his empty stomach ground together. The mountain of unopened mail lay in the same neatly sorted stacks on Kirk's desk, still untouched.

Jeb's temple throbbed. The cord in the back of his neck tightened, and he reached up and rubbed it with his tanned hand.

Kirk hadn't come back.

It could only mean one thing—trouble.

He slammed the door shut and strode back toward Mario. Jeb's dark face and black hair were streaked with sweat and dirt. The grimy stuff coated his narrow shotgun chaps, made of weathered rawhide, and his scuffed black sealskin boots. He took off his black hat and slapped it against his knees, lifting a cloud of choking dust. He could feel dirt and sweat clogging every pore of his massive body. His stomach growled fiercely. More than anything, he wanted to shower and eat.

Hell. He couldn't rest until he found out about Kirk. Megan was the only one on the ranch who might know something.

Jeb had Mario resaddle Caesar, and he swung himself into the saddle, as reluctant as his stallion to gallop back into the hot windy night.

As he rode, Jeb fumed. The MacKays were trouble, more trouble than just about anybody Jeb had ever known, but they were special to him. There was nobody tougher or smarter on the ranch than Kirk MacKay, nobody Jeb admired more. At thirty-five Kirk was three years older than Jeb. As a boy, Jeb had looked up to him, and now he felt closer to MacKay than he did to any of his own brothers.

There was no woman on the ranch tougher or smarter than Megan, either, but that was the problem. She'd had it in for Jeb ever since he'd acquired the MacKay ranch, and she worked double-time to make his life hell. Jeb worked just as hard to avoid her. When he had to be around her he tried not to provoke her, going soft with her, taking her temper tantrums in stride, reminding himself of his fondness for her brother and father, reminding himself that she'd been a favorite playmate of his little sister Julia—before Julia had been kidnapped. Not that his generosity had ever done a lick of good. The nicer Jeb was, the meaner Megan was.

Still, Jeb felt a bond with the MacKays. For more than a hundred years MacKays and Jacksons had stood side by side in south Texas, fighting Indians, defending their cattle from Mexican rustlers, fighting the Yankees during the Confederate War and ranching. Once the MacKay Ranch had been even bigger than the Jackson Ranch, but there had been a wildness in the MacKays that the Jacksons lacked. When the frontier was conquered and the profitable cattle drives of the late nineteenth century were over, when cattle prices had plummeted, the MacKays had been reluctant to settle down and adopt modern methods of ranching. Slowly, acre by acre, the Jacksons had acquired the MacKays' ranch.

Jeb frowned. Why the hell couldn't Kirk be content with being manager of the ranch's quarter-horse program. He was the best horseman Jeb had ever known. Why did Kirk have to get involved in these so-called missions of mercy? Hell, hadn't he retired from the CIA because he was sick of that sort of stuff?

Jeb knew it wasn't the money alone that induced Kirk to risk his life time and again and sneak into foreign countries to free hostage victims. Kirk felt personally responsible for every kidnapping victim in the world. The feeling dated back to when Julia had been kidnapped as a child. She'd been out riding with Kirk, and although Kirk had been only fifteen and the kidnappers had beaten him when he'd fought to defend her, he'd blamed himself. Julia had never been found.

When Jeb reached the MacKay house, he dismounted and tied up Caesar. The house was black and silent, but Jeb knocked loudly on the door just in case. When there was no answer, he lifted the garage door.

The wind sent a page of newsprint fluttering across the empty floor. Jeb let the door fall shut again. He lit a cigarette, and the wind swirled away sparks and the plume of acrid smoke. It was his first one in hours. Jeb took another deep drag.

It was a bad habit, smoking, one he was determined to quit. He just kept putting it off. He'd been putting off a lot of things lately, like asking Janelle to marry him.

Where the hell was Megan, anyway? It wasn't odd that she wasn't home. What was strange was that her car was gone. Megan was quite popular with men and had a date most evenings. Where had she gone alone?

Jeb remembered the roar of the plane flying low, and the familiar knot in his gut tightened.

He tossed his cigarette away and went over to Caesar and untied him. "No use both of us staying up all night," he whispered into his stallion's cocked ear. Caesar's head swiveled viciously, and Jeb had to side-step so Caesar couldn't bite him. Jeb swatted the horse on the rump, and gravel flew as he galloped toward the stable.

Jeb hunkered down in the darkness to wait. In the blackness he listened to a coyote's lonely yelp. Nearby a huisache branch scratched a windowpane.

Half an hour later, at a sound from the road, Jeb threw his second cigarette to the ground, stubbed it out with his boot and crouched in the shadows.

A Blazer with its lights off inched its way cautiously into the caliche drive. Megan!

Her automatic garage door opened. She drove inside and cut the engine. The door closed behind her. Jeb listened to her keys jingling as she let herself into her house by way of the side door.

He waited for her to turn on a light. When she didn't, he glanced at his watch.

It was past midnight. What the hell had she been up to driving across his ranch in the dead of night with no lights? He kept remembering that plane, flying low in the dark, and he didn't like the suspicion forming in his mind.

He stomped his cowboy boots across the front porch and banged so loudly on the door that the clapboard house shook.

When she didn't answer, Jeb started yelling. She seemed to ignore that, too.

"Megan MacKay, you'd better answer this door. If you don't—I'll kick it down."

He paused and listened. The house seemed like a living thing, holding its breath, waiting.

There was no sound, not even a delicate tiptoeing on creaky flooring that would indicate she was at least mildly curious, no sound other than the huisache branch scratching a windowpane.

"Damn mule of a woman!" Jeb thundered. "Megan!" This was a shout much louder than the others.

But there was only silence. And darkness. And the huisache branch. And hot humid gusts blowing dust in his face. The muscle in Jeb's neck screamed with pain.

Damnation! He drew back his boot and measured the distance between his right foot and the door. He'd broken a toe once. It still throbbed every time a norther blew through. He decided on his left foot instead.

Just as the heel of his boot was about to slam into wood, suddenly, unexpectedly, the door flew open. He pitched forward into the black, rectangular hole that gaped as uninvitingly as the opening of a dark cave.

Jeb couldn't see her in the darkness as he stumbled, but he felt her smoldering presence. He caught her fragrance, the scent of wild rose blossoms on a hot summer night.

He half expected her to jump him in the dark.

His stomach clawed.

He stepped further inside.

"Evening," he drawled mildly.

He could have cut the hostile silence with a knife.

There was only the sound of his boots shuffling clumsily on hardwood floors as he groped along one wall for the light switch.

She could have helped him, but she didn't.

"What are you doing here?" she whispered breathlessly. Her voice was velvet-soft, fluid and husky like the dark. Inviting.

His insides tingled. Funny that he'd never noticed before how warm and sexy, how sensual the sound of her voice was.

"I'll ask the questions," he replied roughly. He closed the door and flipped on the light.

"Just go," came that startling, honey-toned whisper, stirring him as it never had before.

He turned toward her and blinked in disbelief.

She was dazzling. Or was it just the sudden brilliance?

He stared hard at the tall, slim woman with her blazing, sea-green eyes and fiery tangles of thick red hair spilling over her shoulders, at this strange yet familiar woman-child who wore nothing but her brother's rumpled green cowboy shirt.

Jeb Jackson had known Megan MacKay all her life.

He was seeing her for the first time.

His eyes followed the vertical curve of her neck. Through the thin green-plaid material of her shirt he could see that her small, high-tipped breasts were alive with indignation. His hands itched to mold their shape, and he clenched them at his side so tightly that they ached. Her honey-colored legs were long and graceful. She was aglow, as if some fierce inner emotion illuminated her.

Never before had her strong, bold beauty so completely commanded his attention. Never had a woman seemed more furiously, more majestically, erotic.

Had he gone crazy? It was the middle of the night. This was only Megan—part brat and all hellion. All he could think of was that she was wearing nothing but that thin shirt that came only halfway to her knees, that they were alone, that it had been forever since he'd had a woman.

A mad pulse throbbed in his temple. His loins were hot. He backed warily toward the door, instinctively reacting to her wildly mussed beauty, to the pleading terror and vulnerability in her eyes, angry at himself and at her because of the uncontrollable feelings.

"If you're staying, I'd better change," she said defiantly.

His black eyes ran over her. Usually she wore her hair tied back in a knot or a ponytail with tailored, drably colored clothes. Jeb had never seen Megan as she was tonight, her beauty rumpled and gloriously flamboyant, like some wind-tossed blossom on a stormy night.

"I like you just the way you are," he murmured.

Her vivid eyes shot sparks at him. She pressed her lips tightly together, and he was grateful she was silent.

He knew that fiery-eyed look. It was damned cute and filled him with a strange hunger. But it meant she was going to be obstinate. He turned away and studied the familiar room in which he'd spent so many enjoyable hours when he was a boy. Megan had loved him then, idolized him even, but that had been before her father had lost the ranch to Jeb. The room was plainly furnished with the heavy furniture the vaqueros had built on the ranch for all of its cottages.

On a narrow shelf there were small carved wooden figures that depicted various aspects of ranch life. There was a horse and rider, a cowboy whirling a lariat, a windmill and a roadrunner. Graceful figures, lovingly made. Glen had whittled them. There was one in particular that Jeb had always fancied, but Megan had refused to give it to him. It was of Jeb and Megan walking together, holding hands. Her skirt and hair were blowing. Jeb could almost feel the cool wind and remember the smell of the wildflowers in that meadow, of the wildflowers in her hair. Megan had adored him then. That was before she'd decided he was the one who'd ruined her life.

Jeb turned back to Megan. She was as beautiful as before, and it was still as much of a shock to him.

He felt his will, his reliable, indomitable will, dissolving at the sight of her. It was as though her luminous beauty had invaded every male cell of his body.

She was strangely silent, as if she, too, were lost and uncertain and warily afraid to make the wrong move.

He watched her, noticing how her skin reflected the golden light, how her eyes flashed and shimmered with lovely violent-soft green fires. She made him feel young again; she filled him with a nostalgic yearning for things he hadn't dreamed of in years. There had always been something missing in his life, something wonderful, half dreamed of, mysterious, lacking in his relationships with his passive, understanding women. That something had been missing even during the brief contentment of his marriage.

He lost himself in the fire of Megan's jewel-green eyes. The world seemed new. He felt wild, totally unlike himself.

"What do you want?" she whispered.

He looked at her with a fresh ache in his gut. His eyes burned, touching her intimately. He wanted to slide his hands down her spine and over her hips and pull her body close so that it curved tightly into his.

He caught a sharp breath. "Where's Kirk?"

She took a faltering step back. The light flowed out of her eyes and drained from her cheeks. She looked exactly as she had the night her father had run off.

She was afraid, in a way Jeb hadn't often seen her afraid, and the fear no longer had to do only with him. He felt himself softening toward her.

"I don't know," she whispered, looking away into a dark corner.

Jeb sighed. "I can see this is a battle that could go on all night." He pulled his pack of cigarettes from his shirt pocket and shook one into his palm.

"You know I don't approve of smoking."

He shrugged indifferently. His lighter flared, and he inhaled deeply. They both watched a large puff of his smoke invade the virgin territory of the MacKay house, he with satisfaction, she with an anger that brought color flooding back into her face.

"You don't approve of me, period," he said. "Would you mind making me a cup of coffee?"

"I'm not one of your servants at the Big House."

His eyes skimmed over her. He smiled sardonically. "You can say that again."

A swift, hot flush rose in her cheeks. He took his
hat off and tossed it on her couch. She frowned at the
cloud of dust that burst forth from the Stetson. Then
he marched to her kitchen and began to throw open
cabinet doors and rummage through the contents of
her drawers. He smoked while he dug through her
things. She opened two windows, and the sweet night
smells of mesquite and the range drifted inside.

Arms stiffly folded over her breasts, she watched
him in mulish, stormy silence. At last she could stand
it no longer.

"You could at least wash your hands. I'm going to
have to scrub the woodwork for hours."

"That's a problem you could have avoided." He
threw a wad of herbal tea bags onto the counter.

She dug her nails into her elbows.

"I'd forgotten you were a health nut," he growled.

"Just because I don't believe in killing myself with
nicotine and caffeine, that makes me a health nut?"

He shot her a charming, lopsided grin. "Damn
right."

As he searched through her pantry, three cans fell
off a shelf onto the linoleum floor.

"You can't just go through my things," she sput-
tered, stopping a rolling can with her bare toe.

"I'll quit, if you'll just show me where Kirk keeps
his coffee."

Studying a black handprint on her yellow cupboard, Megan surrendered. Silently she opened the refrigerator, pulled out a fresh can and set it down with a clank beside the can opener. Jeb picked up the can and smiled broadly into her scowling face. With swift, silent expertise he opened the coffee and started it perking.

"You have no right to come to my house...."

"My house," he murmured silkily, "remember?" His eyes raked over her. "Everything on this ranch belongs to me." Just the smell of the coffee perking rejuvenated him. He focused his full attention on Megan. "Where were you tonight?" he demanded softly.

"I guess that's my business."

"Maybe. Maybe it's my business, too."

Her eyes met his briefly. "You may own this house, but you don't own me."

He put his cigarette down and smiled at her. "You're always saying things like that, Megan. You like to taunt me with your independence. Sometimes I wonder why. Is it because you don't quite believe in it?"

"N-no."

He laughed softly, liking the way the desire-tinged sound threatened her. She was trembling, clinging to the refrigerator door handle, letting it go, backing into the darkness, not wanting him to see her reaction.

He moved toward her, cornering her in the dark pocket behind the refrigerator. She was a tall woman, but his immense, muscled body dwarfed hers. He liked feeling her so close just as he liked feeling that she was trapped unless he chose to let her go. The passionate fire in her eyes burned him, excited him. She seemed soft and delicate and feminine, but at the same time wild. He held back from touching her, but only because he wanted to so badly. But he felt the nearness of her, the heat of her skin that burned a degree or two hotter than other women's, the warmth of her breath stirring the air. She aroused him as no woman ever had.

"There's some around here who'd say you were mine," he murmured. "I remember the time even you thought so."

Jeb didn't know why he was deliberately rankling her. He was only making trouble for himself. But some demon in him wanted passion from her tonight even if it was nothing more than anger.

"You never intend to let me forget that night, do you?"

"It was quite a night. A night like that is hard for a man to forget," he said huskily. "How many times are there in a man's life that he wins a ranch and a woman, too, in a game of five-card stud?"

"Damn you." She closed her eyes as if to hide from the bitter memory. Then they flashed open once more. "You tricked my father into gambling with you that night."

Jeb chuckled softly. "No, honey. I just beat him."

"I was barely sixteen."

"You were all woman. Sometimes I think you were born that way."

"I was asleep, and you let Daddy gamble away the ranch."

"He knew what he was doing."

"When I woke up you had the deed as well as guardianship papers for me. Daddy was gone. You drove him away."

Jeb's black eyes were stony in his set face. "You're wrong about that."

"Kirk should have killed you when he came back from the Middle East. I don't know why he didn't."

"Because he likes me. Because he likes working for me. Because he knew I'd take better care of you than your own family ever did."

"That's a lie."

"You only wish it was!"

"You're a bastard, Jeb Jackson, for not letting that memory die."

"Am I?" he purred, closing in on her. "I've always wondered which made you madder—me winning you, or me turning you down that night when you offered yourself to me? Maybe you were only sixteen, but you damn sure knew how to seduce a man."

She drew back her hand to slap him, but he grabbed both wrists and yanked her closer.

She struggled breathlessly. "I hate you."

"But did you then?" He chuckled. She was on fire, and he was consumed by her. "I thought of you as my little sister back then, but it was no secret that you'd had a high-school crush on me for years. Maybe that was my fault. I kept coming around because you reminded me of Julia. I thought it was cute the way you tried to flirt with me."

Every word infuriated her. She'd hated him for years, and he was teasing her, making fun of her, taking away the one thing he had never fully robbed her of before—her pride.

Her fingers curved into the hard muscles of his chest, and had his hands not tightened on her wrists, she would have sunk her nails into his flesh.

"No, my little wildcat," he whispered, bending her body closer against his huge length. "I'll not endure your scratches, too."

She twisted against him, but her every movement only made her body slide more sensually against his. He was hot and tired and dirty, but he was all man. She had grown up on a ranch, and the smell of tobacco and leather and horses, sweat and dust, were powerful masculine scents to her. Wide-shouldered and lean even in his filthy work clothes, his rugged features made handsome by his rakish and slightly crooked grin...

Megan felt herself melting and becoming even hotter against him. He felt it, too, and his touch gentled. Though he still held her locked to his sleek, hot body, he did so effortlessly, tracing her backbone with his fingertips. At last she lay against him quietly, defeated.

A vast silence stretched between them.

She was almost his height, and through his cotton shirt he felt the faint pressure of her nipples tightening against his own. Her heart pounded against his heart with the same too-rapid rhythm. He felt her heat flowing into him and knew the hunger he felt was in her, too.

Coltishly her hands came up and she let her fingers glide in wonder over his shoulders and his chest and down to his waist, exploring the unfamiliar male shapes and bulges, the sinewy muscles of his arms, and the hardness and massive width of his chest. She stopped at his waistband, realizing the enormity of what she had done, and yanked her hands to her side.

"Sometimes I think I should have taken you that night even though you were just a half-grown kid," he rasped thickly into her hair. "I think I could have won you more easily in the bedroom than I've ever been able to by offering you friendship."

She tried to push him away, and he loosened his hold but didn't let her go entirely.

"Friendship?" She arched her brows. "Is that what you call it? You were a tyrant."

His hands were in her hair, trying to smooth it, discovering it couldn't be smoothed. "Because I wouldn't let you run away. Because I made you go to school. Because I wouldn't let you date just anybody. Because I wouldn't let you marry that bum. I was your legal guardian. It was my responsibility to try to straighten you out.''

''And you take all your responsibilities so seriously.''

''Like I just said, maybe I should have taken you to bed.''

''I would have only hated you more.''

He laughed. ''So what?'' His fingers touched her beneath her chin, trailed down her throat until she shivered. ''Hatred is a fascinating emotion in you, almost an attractive one. Why, Megan, you're trembling.''

''With disgust,'' she whispered, frantic.

A callused fingertip touched her again, lightly tracing the pulse that throbbed with the fever of her heart. A tremor raced through her. He watched the quick, hot blood of shame seep into her cheeks.

''I'm not so sure. Do the men you date make you tremble and blush just by touching you?'' His hand tightened possessively. He could feel her pulse ticking more erratically. The thought of other men putting their hands on the satin gold of her skin was distinctly unpleasant. Suddenly Jeb understood the swift, hot urge that could compel men to murder.

''Of course not!'' she replied, deeply shocked. ''I don't hate them like I hate you.''

He smiled, a slow, subtle movement that curved

his lips but did not disturb the hard steel of his eyes. "I'm beginning to think the reason you date so many different men is because you've never dated one that makes you feel like a woman."

"My love life is none of your business," she whispered.

"I've decided to make it my business." His voice hardened. "That new Dr. Ferguson comes around a lot."

"I'm not going to discuss Byrom with you. Just because you're the boss of Jackson Ranch, you think you're king of the county."

"So it's Byrom." Jeb forced a laugh. "And it's five counties, honey."

She glared at him with eyes as bright as gemstones. "Well, the king part was right," she muttered bitterly. "Only I should have said bully."

"Why do you persist in hating me, Megan? No weakling could run a ranch like this. And a real bastard would have taken advantage of you, a raw furious kid that night. You were cute, and you'd been chasing me for years. A bastard wouldn't have brought you to his home, endured your tantrums and sulky moods for ten years, educated you, paid for your flying lessons, hired you as the ranch's pilot. I treated you like a sister. Your own flesh and blood never did half for you what I've done."

"Whatever you did, Jeb Jackson, you owed me.

You stole my father's ranch. You even had the gall to turn it into a game ranch.''

"That's the only way I could figure to make that miserable scrap of heavily mortgaged land pay."

"That miserable scrap of land was my home," she snapped.

"I've given you a home."

"That was little enough since it was you who drove my father off!"

"The hell I did! I…"

"Are you going to talk all night, Jeb? Or are you going to leave so I can get a decent night's sleep?"

"I'm not going anywhere till you tell me where Kirk is." Jeb's voice was low, but dangerous.

Panic welled in her eyes.

He grabbed her by the arms and brought her face so near his own she flinched. "The sooner you tell me, the sooner you get rid of me."

Her eyes widened, but she shook her head obstinately.

"You're not just angry. You're scared. And being scared always makes you madder. Kirk's in trouble isn't he?" Jeb paused. "And when Kirk finds trouble, he can get into one hell of a jam. Megan, honey…" Jeb's voice softened, and when it did, he felt her body soften in his arms. "I remember one time in Mexico…"

At the word "Mexico" her eyes grew even wilder and she jerked loose of his grip. "You're having fun, aren't you? Acting as if you like me. Playing with me.''

"I'm not playing."

"Well, I can't tell you. It doesn't matter how you play with my emotions. Don't you understand?" Her voice was raw and agonized. "Kirk's life depends on my silence."

His own voice was just as agonized. "Megan, what the hell is going on?"

She shook her head silently.

"You little fool! You were out tonight, trying to save him! I heard the plane. I saw you driving home across the ranch without lights!"

She shook her head again, and when she did, he saw a crooked slash along her hairline that had been hidden by her hair. He pulled her closer, his brown fingers sifting through the fiery coils as he examined the jagged cut.

With a savage gesture, he let her go. "So that's why your hair's down. You were deliberately hiding this from me. What the hell happened to your face?"

Her eyes flickered fearfully across his hard, male features. "You can bully everybody else on this ranch, but not me."

"Oh, that again." His jaw tightened. The lines beside his lips grew taut and white. "Damn it. Can't you see I want to help you?" He longed to shake her, to thrash her.

She smiled at the violence she read in his eyes. "Hit me! Go ahead. It'd be just like you!"

He drew a long breath and got a grip on his temper. "Megan, I know you've somehow gotten yourself involved in one of Kirk's missions. You're probably in way over your head. He's an ex-CIA agent, one of the best there ever was. He can take care of himself. I'm not so sure you can, if things are as desperate as they are beginning to appear. Whatever you think of me, you know Kirk is my closest friend. There's nothing I wouldn't do to help him."

"Jeb Jackson, you're the last man on earth I'd come to if I were in trouble. The very last."

The old hate and suspicion were in her eyes, and it hurt him somehow, more than it ever had.

"But you're not the one in trouble, honey. Kirk is. And I'm the first man he'd come to. Remember that, Megan. I can fly damn nearly as well as you can. It's stupid to go down there without a qualified copilot. If anything happens to him, you'll have that on your conscience for the rest of your life."

Megan shivered, shrinking from Jeb's hard expression. Her gaze flew guiltily about the room and then back to him. "Look, there's just no way I can trust you. Not after all you've done. And I'm not going to risk your trying to stop me. Just go."

Jeb felt a cold, all-consuming fury toward her. Hell, he'd never known how to handle her.

"All right," he muttered angrily. "For now. Since you're getting more stubborn by the minute. But I'll be back. You can count on it."

Three

___

Saturday was another white hot day, just as Jeb had known it would be, and it seemed to stick to him as he got out of his air-conditioned blue Cadillac. He strode across the slab of concrete outside the hangar where Megan's yellow and white Piper Cub was tied down beside his Mooney and his Lear jet.

It was hours till noon, but the wind was already starting to come up. Megan was hosing her plane down, and for a second, before she saw him, he stopped and watched her. He was tired in every bone in his body, but she was a pretty sight with her thick, red hair bunched into a pony tail, with her slim body encased in faded jeans and a pink knit top.

For a skinny girl, she had a cute bottom.

Megan turned her back to him, and water splashed onto the pavement as she inspected her landing gear. Even from a distance he could see her bruised cheek and the vividly cruel scarlet slash against her hairline. He still wanted to know what in the name of hell had happened to her face.

He walked up quietly behind her. The hose was on the ground, staining the concrete a darker color as it gushed out his precious well water full blast. Megan was running her fingers carefully along a crooked strut. The paint was scratched and flaking, and there was gooey black clay on the landing gear.

What had happened to her plane?

He'd find out if it was the last thing he did.

Megan bent lower, and blue denim strained over her female shape. Suddenly Jeb wasn't thinking about the damaged Piper or about his gushing well water or about Kirk. Instead, Jeb's gaze was rivetted to the curvaceous tilt of Megan's shapely backside.

He had dreamed about her last night. Dreamed about having her naked in his bed between his sheets, dreamed about her crawling on top of him, dreamed of her kissing him passionately, dreamed about her going limp and quivering all over when he kissed her back. He had tasted her, made love to her, and she'd tasted like honeyed wine and burned like flame. He'd awakened in a cold sweat with an ache in his gut, and the ache had been very different from the usual knot of frustration she aroused in him. He'd lain in bed for hours after that, thinking about her, wanting her, and wishing he didn't.

It was a perverse twist of fate that made him want a woman who hated him with a fierce, implacable fury that had lasted ten years.

Something had happened to him in the MacKay cottage last night, something he hadn't asked for, hadn't expected and didn't want. If there was one thing Jeb Jackson had learned in the thirty-two years he'd lived, it was that powerful feelings brought powerful consequences.

He didn't want Megan MacKay getting a grip on him. He wanted things to be as they'd always been. Megan MacKay was supposed to be his brat sister, someone he put up with, someone he looked after because he had to, someone he ignored most of the time.

She bent lower, and her bottom tilted higher—invitingly.

Heat poured into his loins, and he couldn't stop looking at her. There was no panty line. Shining spirals of red hair streamed over her backbone like flame. She was braless, too. Not that she was the bosomy sort that couldn't go without a bra. Still, when a woman didn't wear underwear, it made her seem freer. It made a man wonder. Just how free would she be in his bed? Jeb wondered, too, if she knew he was there, if she was only pretending not to know, if she'd

gotten into that position deliberately to torment him.
It would be just like her. Or was it something she just
did all the time? Positioning herself so that any man
who saw her would want to grab her and pull her
under his body? Suddenly Jeb stopped and searched
the hangar angrily for Lauro, but luckily for Lauro,
the man was discreetly out of sight, probably because
he'd seen the boss and wanted Jeb to think he was
busy.

Jeb moved closer. He wanted to touch her, to pull
her into his arms, to taste her as he had done in his
dream.

"Planning another little trip tonight?" he drawled
sardonically.

Megan couldn't have jumped higher if a snake's
fangs had sunk into her big toe.

So she really hadn't known he was there.

She whirled around. Her green eyes were enormous, unfriendly, passionately afraid.

His own feelings were equally intense. He was
aware of a pulse in his throat throbbing like the wildest jungle drum.

She was beautiful with the muted sunlight in her
hair, all honey and fire, exactly as she'd been in his
dream. Hungrily he imagined her naked. She would
be long-legged and graceful rather than voluptuous.
Golden-colored, all over. She would give a man fire
instead of the sweetness Jeb's women had always
given him.

Maybe that was it. Maybe he just wanted something different. Before he settled down for good.

One last fling before marriage.

Whatever, he wanted this insane urge for Megan MacKay to pass quickly—before it got him into big trouble.

Megan jerked her hose up from the ground and splashed water onto a wing.

He had asked her if she were planning another little trip, Jeb remembered.

"No," she replied. Her single word was bitten out.

"It's a bad habit, wasting water, when you live in a desert," he said smoothly, knowing the remark would rile her.

"I'll pay for it," she snapped, whirling back to him.

Her hair was a banner of flame. Her eyes burned him.

But he wanted her fire.

"It's still a bad habit," he drawled lazily.

"I've got lots of them."

"Don't we all?" He grinned. "Bad habits make a woman more interesting. But I'm sure you know that."

Her eyes flashed. "What did you come out here for?"

He moved closer. He smiled when she stood her ground. He liked her staying close. "Are you planning your trip for tomorrow night, then?"

Megan stiffened with alarm. "What I do on my own time in my own plane is my own business." The water was rushing onto the concrete again.

"Not when it's illegal," he murmured softly. "Not when you're doing it on my ranch. I'm going to find out what you're up to. Last night several of the vaqueros heard a plane flying low over the ranch, but when they looked up they saw no lights. They figured it was a drug dealer's plane. I heard it myself. Lauro said you landed your Piper at ten o'clock. I figure it was you we heard."

Jeb was so close he could have touched her. He wanted to. He wanted to know if she would tremble again, if he had only imagined her trembling last night.

She remembered the water and began to spray the Piper again. "Leave it alone, Jeb. It's none of your business."

His handsome face was very hard, very male. His voice was just as hard. "It is when a federal agent calls me and says he's got a warrant and wants to search my ranch."

"What?"

Lauro stepped out of the hangar, and Jeb shouted to him, "Hey, Lauro, cut the damned water off."

Lauro did.

Jeb turned back to Megan. "I just got off the phone. They think someone on this ranch is running drugs."

She glared at the useless nozzle of her hose and then flung it to the ground. "Th-that's ridiculous."

"That's what I told them. I said I'd look into the matter personally, and if I discovered anything amiss I'd inform them immediately. I gave them my word."

"And?" She tossed her head back with an air of bravado, and her ponytail swung freely in the wind.

"They agreed, of course."

He wanted to take her hair down, to crush its thickness, its wildness, its sweetness, in his hands, as he wanted to crush her slim body against his own.

"Naturally," she said. "Doesn't anyone ever stand up to you?"

"There is one person." Black eyes glanced off defiant green ones. "I would have thought you'd be pleased this place won't be crawling with feds."

She shrugged her shoulders in an attempt at nonchalance. "Why should I care?"

He wanted to grab her and shake her but was afraid to because he wanted to touch her so badly. He balled his hands into fists and jammed them deeply into his pockets. "You might find it difficult to explain certain facts," he replied.

"Such as?"

"You flew to Mexico last night, and back." He ground out the sentence. "Illegally. The feds were hot on your tail when your plane landed on this ranch. They were tracking you with airborne radar. You didn't file a flight plan. You didn't communicate with ground control. If information on that unauthorized flight were to get out to the right people, I hate to think how quickly you'd lose all of your licenses.''

''And of course you know all the right people, and I'm totally in your power.'' Her voice was unsteady, and she was shaking.

He had her where he wanted her—scared—and yet if he were so all-fire powerful, why was he afraid to take her in his arms, why was he afraid she would try to slap him again as she had last night?

''Of course, that's me—all-powerful,'' he said quietly, ironically.

''And you'd do it, too! Just to get your way! Everybody and everything has got to be under the thumb of King Jackson.''

He laughed. ''Why should I bother defending myself? It never gets me anywhere with you. Besides, it's a pleasant thought—having you under my thumb.''

He held out his hands, pointing his thumbs toward her, and she jumped back.

He laughed, and then as he looked at her, he stopped laughing.

There was a profound silence between them as he moved closer, backing her against the plane. The familiar ache was in his gut as he studied her; it was stronger, hotter than ever before. He had only to edge closer, to touch her.

He stood with his legs apart, looming over her like

some monumental colossus. His eyes roved the length of her body, sliding over her green eyes and wild, red hair that cascaded against her slender neck, lingering on her swelling breasts straining against the pink cotton-knit shirt. His gaze moved lower, tracing her narrow waist and the long, sleek curves of her thighs and hips in her tight, revealing jeans.

Hot, furious color raced into her cheeks, making her more enticingly beautiful than ever.

She drew a deep breath. So did he.

Their eyes met, and for a long charged moment neither spoke.

Hemmed in against the plane, there was nowhere she could run. She felt defeated, lost, afraid, and there was some new feeling, something worse than all the others. Wisps of flame-colored hair blew about her face as she struggled under the grip of this new, unwanted emotion.

He didn't understand what she felt, but he saw it. He watched her brush at her eyes as if she were afraid of tears. Her hand was trembling. For once, Megan seemed afraid to speak.

Her eyes glistened, but no tears fell. He'd known her all her life and he'd never seen her cry. Not when her wild, half-Comanche mother had run off with that man. Not even when her father had disappeared and she'd lost her ranch. Not when Jeb had turned her former childhood home into a hunting lodge for his friends. Not even now when Kirk's life hung in the balance, and she was terrified.

She squared her shoulders and tilted her chin back.

He wished he didn't want her. He wished he'd never heard that plane, never gone to her cottage last night. He wished it was Janelle he wanted like this.

Megan was the wrong woman.

Yet never had he felt more powerfully drawn to another.

Maybe it was her hatred that fascinated him. Maybe it had been eating away at him, bit by bit, getting inside him, without his knowing it was. Maybe it was just the challenge of her. He hoped that's all it was. He hoped this new insane fascination would die a quick death.

But if it didn't, whatever he did, Jeb had to keep her from knowing how powerfully she aroused him, because if she knew, she'd only use it as a weapon against him.

"A man could boil alive out here today," he murmured, knowing that it wasn't the heat of the day that was beading his brow with sweat and making his shirt stick to him. "Be in my office in an hour," he said. "And you'd better tell me the truth. Or it's no more job. No more airplanes. Ever. You can continue living on Jackson Ranch, of course. I never go back on my word, and I promised your father you'd always have a home here. But that's all you'll have."

Her face went white, her hair seemed a lurid orange

in contrast, and her eyes looked like green bits of hot glitter.

No ordinary man with a grain of sense would have turned his back on a woman who looked at him like that.

He turned, readjusted his Stetson. Then he let long, arrogant strides carry him quickly toward his Cadillac.

But not quickly enough.

Megan, lithe and slim-legged, chased after him. She was shaking. Her pale face was luminous with hatred. Her voice vibrated with charged emotion. "Don't you dare turn your back on me, you coward."

"Coward?" He swore viciously to himself as he turned slowly to face her. Beneath the wide-brimmed Stetson, his dark face was half-shadowed, unreadable.

"Your word?" she cried, and the harsh sound of her voice tore at him.

His expression hardened.

"As if you've ever been a man of honor." She tried to laugh, but all she could manage was a hoarse, choked sound.

He saw the anguish in her eyes, and he forgot his own fear. Her anguish was his.

"You stole my home, drove my father away, bossed me around for years and murdered the wild animals that had roamed MacKay land as tamely as pets. Now you're threatening to make sure I never fly again. Flying's all I've got. I can't stand the way you use the power you have over me! This is blackmail! You're worse than any rattler. Vile! You'll do anything to get what you want. Anything!''

His dark eyes met her contemptuous gaze. He wanted to take her in his arms, to kiss her violently until she wanted him as much as he wanted her. The desire to do so was a hot, ungovernable force. He could feel his hands shaking, and it made him furious at himself, at her, that she could drive him so wild.

She hated him. What wouldn't she do if she knew she had him in the palm of her hand—right where she'd always wanted him?

He steeled himself. He let his gaze narrow cynically. His voice was harsh. ''I thought you figured that out ten years ago the night I won you and your ranch. I play to win, Megan. I always have. And I always will.''

He was mad to have her, to comfort her, to help her.

He turned away.

She thought only that he was so arrogant he'd decided to coolly ignore her, as if she and the wrongs he'd done her were nothing. He thought of her as a possession he could use any way he wanted to. She was one of the little people on the ranch where he was king.

Watching those broad shoulders move so coolly and haughtily away from her made something inside Megan break. She wanted to scream, to cry out, to strike out at him. But she knew he was so high above her, she could never really hurt him, and she struggled to control herself.

What was so different about today? About this moment? Hadn't the Jacksons been taking things and crushing people for a hundred years? It was all a game to Jeb. *She* was a game to him. Nothing more. She'd never mattered to him. Nor had her father's ranch. Jeb had simply wanted the ranch to extend his hunting acreage, so he'd taken it, not caring that he'd broken up her family. And now it was her brother's life he was playing with. Jeb didn't care about Kirk. Not really. Kirk was just useful to him. Like a windmill. Or an oil well. Or a champion bull. Like Caesar, that damned mean horse he'd paid a million dollars for, that went around biting hunks out of people, even Jeb. To Jeb, Kirk wasn't even as valuable as any of those.

It was the Jackson way: to want, to take, to rule.

Megan stared after Jeb in impotent, raging fury.

She hadn't slept last night. Her old nightmare had come back to haunt her. She'd been afraid. For Kirk. Of Jeb finding out. Of Jeb somehow figuring out a way to stop her from going after Kirk.

But there was this new feeling, too. She kept remembering the way Jeb had touched her last night, the strange, terrible way he'd made her feel. It had happened again when he'd backed her up against her plane. It was like she'd been a kid all over again, hungry for his love, wanting him again like she had back then, and him not really wanting her, just teasing her because it suited his ego, just playing with her as if she were some kind of new toy. Only now she wasn't a kid. Now she knew that for all his money and power he was no good. He was greedy and selfish and just plain hateful. He'd pretended to be her father's friend. Jeb had taken everything that had ever mattered to her.

Oh, why did he have to be so ruggedly good-looking with those hot, devil-black eyes? Why was he so hard and tall and dark? Even last night when he'd been sweaty and filthy, she'd thought him the most handsome man alive. He was masculine to the core. There was a coiled intensity in him, as if he'd lived his whole life without ever letting go. She wanted to know what he'd be like if he ever did.

Why couldn't she forget how his eyes had burned last night every time he'd looked at her? Megan knew the ranch needed money and that Jeb had a rich cousin in California and that he was planning to marry her the way he'd married that other rich girl when he'd needed money.

Megan knew there had never been any gossip about Jeb fooling around with women on a casual basis, but she'd always figured that was only because Jeb was so low-down and greedy he never took a serious interest in a woman unless she had acres and acres of rich ranch land and barrels and barrels of oil.

Jeb kept on walking toward his car as if he'd totally forgotten Megan.

Megan's eyes stabbed daggers into that broad, muscled back. Her emotions seemed to mingle and blur as they built in power. She felt pushed and afraid, terribly confused, too near the edge not to fall over.

Never in all her life had she even come close to hysteria. But it welled up in her now, choking her, making her forget her pride.

He was going to take her licenses away! Kirk might die!

She kept watching the cocky tilt of Jeb's Stetson and the infuriatingly sensual cowboy swagger of male hips in tight denim as he strode toward his car.

He was lean and hard and indifferent.

She ached to hurt him as she was hurting. To take him down a notch. To make him know fear as she knew it. To make him lose that careful veneer of cool control. To make him know the fierce, swift pain of hot, uncontrollable passion as she knew it. To make him know that he was only a man and not some god above it all.

Scarcely knowing what she did, she ran after him, lunging at him when she caught up to him, attacking him, but his body was rock-hard from his outdoor life. Her puny blows fell weakly against his muscled back. All she succeeded in doing was to knock his hat onto the ground.

"What the hell?" Jeb whirled around and clasped her to him.

Just for a second she wondered where Lauro was, if he and the other mechanic were watching her make a fool of herself.

Then she forgot everything but Jeb. She dug her nails into his arms and cried out, using Kirk's military vocabulary in a barrage of creative insults that brought a faint curve to those sensual, cruel lips.

Jeb's callused hands slid gently yet roughly down her arms, running over her trembling body, molding her against himself, forcing her to quiet, controlling her. She clung to him, feeling her hot skin against his heavy, throbbing form.

"You bastard! You damned, cocky bast..."

She lost her voice, lost the ability to shout the wealth of vivid insults that bubbled up from her heart.

As if from a great distance, she heard his low, gravelly, soothing drawl.

"Hush, Megan. Darling... You're hysterical."

His lips were against her ear. In her hair. Against her throat. And she wanted them there, hot and seeking.

"Darling..." The word echoed soothingly somewhere in her ravaged brain. She felt his hands caressing her, running through her hair. She felt the strength of him flowing into her tired, drained body, the warmth of him.

''N-no. I'm not hysterical,'' she sobbed. ''I'm not!''

Her tears were strangling her. When she tried to speak, only disjointed sounds came forth. He kissed her eyelids, her fevered brow, and she clung to him.

He was so tough. Yet so gentle.

She wasn't hysterical! Why were the tears running freely from her eyes? She could feel them scalding her cheeks. She turned her face from his, not wanting him to see.

But he saw her terrible vulnerability, and instead of laughing at her in triumph as she expected him to, his dark, rugged face was gravely tender. It almost made her forget who he was, all that he'd done.

''There's never been anyone, not anyone except Kirk for me,'' she murmured.

''I know,'' came that unbelievably gentle male tone.

''He's all I have. Everybody else, everything else is gone. First Julia, and Kirk blaming himself for it. Then Mother. After that Kirk went away and joined the Marines, then the CIA. When he came back he was so hard and bitter. You took our ranch and Daddy went away. Everybody said the MacKays were wild and no good. It seems like I've always been alone. And never more than now!''

Jeb's hands felt so warm as they caressed her neck. All the hot, angry feelings flowed out of her. ''Kirk could be dying. Maybe he's already dead. I don't know what to do. I feel so alone. There's no one I can turn to. You don't know what it's like, not having things or people in your life, not having power. You've always had everything. Family. Money. You were born with it all.''

He thought of the invoices on his desk, the new loans he needed to keep the ranch going, the medical career he'd given up because his father had wanted him to run the ranch. "Did it ever occur to you that people can't help who they're born to, Megan?" Jeb asked softly. "Not even someone as mean and awful as me.''

His irony was lost on her.

Her tear-filled eyes sought his. "I don't care about any of it except for Kirk. Jeb, don't you dare try to stop me from helping him. Don't you dare! I swear I'll kill you if you try to. I'd kill anybody—''

"I'm not going to stop you, Megan. I want to help you. Haven't I always helped you even when you didn't want to be helped?''

His words didn't make sense and yet somehow they did.

"Even if it means breaking laws? You've always been so straitlaced about the law.''

"Honey, I want to save Kirk as much as you do.''

"You could wind up in a Mexican jail.''

"I've been in worse places.''

She knew it was crazy not to push him away, but she held him tighter.

She felt his lips on her cheeks, tasting the saltiness of her tears, and she liked the soft feeling of his hard mouth moving across her hot skin. Nothing in all her life had ever felt so good.

"I've never seen you cry," he said gently.

He had never been so nice, so kind. She had never realized how much she had longed for his kindness.

"I've cried before," she admitted weakly, "lots of times, but when I was alone...because I was too proud to let you know."

"It's nothing to be ashamed of—crying. Most women do, you know."

"I never wanted to be like most women."

"You damn sure succeeded there." He spoke forcefully, but he was smiling at her, too.

She stared into his eyes, and she felt herself drowning in those blazing pools. "I—I don't know what's happening to me," she stammered.

"I don't know, either," he growled fiercely, lowering his mouth to her lips.

"I—I don't want to want you," she whispered against his mouth. She felt his warm breath against her face. "Oh, Jeb, I don't want to."

"The feeling's mutual," he replied grimly, but his hands tightened possessively on her body, and he arched her closer.

Her breasts pressed into his chest, and her own fluttering pulse sped madly.

"Then why?" She gasped. "What are we doing? Have we both gone crazy?"

"Seems like it." Jeb's voice was as soft as velvet. His eyes were deep and dark, concealing his emotions.

"You're going to marry Janelle," Megan reminded him frantically as his lips moved closer. The very thought brought a little moan of pain from her lips.

He frowned, fighting to concentrate on Janelle, but the vision of her soft, cool beauty blurred. The hot fragrance of wild roses filled his nostrils; the longing to taste lush, honeyed lips tempted him. All he could feel was the fire and the wild sweetness of the woman he held in his arms.

"No, honey," he muttered. "I'm going to kiss you."

Megan tried to twist away, but he caught her to him. "It's too late to fight it. Way too late—for both of us." His mouth came down on hers, frightening, greedy in its demand. Yet no greedier than her own.

She could feel his pulse pounding like a savage jungle drum. Her own leapt at the same rhythm. Her hands tightened around his neck, feeling his hard muscles as well as the silken texture of his hair.

He was trembling, and so was she. She could feel the harsh rumble of his ragged breathing, and his wildness was in her as well. They were caught in a storm, lashed by its force. He ground her against his immense body.

What happened was like nothing either of them had ever known before.

Lips slid against lips, flesh against flesh, man against woman, but with an inner magical explosion of primitive sensation that left them both shaken.

He had kissed many women. She had been kissed by other men.

But this was different for them both.

His tongue slid inside her mouth.

One taste, and he knew that every moment in his life had led him to this instant, to this woman. She had always possessed him. He had always fought it. He had always wondered if she could be soft, like other women. He discovered that she was soft, but she was not like other women.

One kiss and he was lost. His two-year courtship of Janelle was as nothing to this. There was only Megan and this moment.

Only Megan, who hated him.

Never had a woman tasted sweeter, wilder.

Abruptly he released her.

But his eyes sought hers.

Her face was still, upturned. Her hair had come loose and was blowing in the wind. In her blazing eyes he saw brief bewilderment. The look was gone in a flash.

She buried her face in her hands, sick with shame to have let him kiss her, to have burst into flame when he had.

"We might as well have that talk in my office now," he muttered, as uncomfortable as she was.

Through her fingers, her eyes sparked with desperation.

He touched her elbow to guide her toward his Cadillac, but she jerked away and raced defiantly ahead of him, opened the car door and hurled herself inside.

He knelt and picked up his hat and slapped it against his thigh.

They drove silently, sitting stiffly beside each other, neither of them speaking, both of them seeking something outside the car to look at.

The scenery was flat desert punctuated by pockets of brush and mesquite. It was too familiar, and it held no interest for either of them. She fiddled with her hair for a while; then she switched on the radio. It was set to his favorite kicker station, and a country singer's melancholy croon filled the car. Megan twirled the dial until she found a rock station.

The tense, metallic twanging seemed to make the taut nerve ends explode in Jeb's brain. He glanced toward her and saw her fingers patting out the rhythm on her knee. He gritted his teeth and endured it.

She turned the volume up.

He was aware of those tapping fingers. It was as if they pounded a tattoo in every nerve cell of his body. What was she trying to do, blast him out of his own car?

He didn't say anything. He just lit a cigarette and took a long drag.

She opened her window.

They drove in mutual misery to his ranch office. When they reached it, they both sprang out of the Cadillac. Their doors slammed in unison.

Inside his office they regarded each other warily. Then she went to the window and looked out as if she were searching for some avenue of escape.

Her silence was oppressive, but Jeb decided there was nothing to do but to launch his attack. "Kirk must be in Mexico, and we've got to risk our own necks to go down and get him out." She glared out the window and pretended to ignore him, so he went on. "You and I have been at war for years. I just kissed you, and you kissed me back. Maybe it shouldn't have happened, but it did. I don't like it any more than you!" Silence. "It's been a helluva morning. I don't usually drink this time of the day, but what would you say to a shot of whiskey?"

She turned stiffly. "What I always say—no."

His mouth quirked. "Sorry I don't have any herbal tea." He poured a glass for her and set it in front of her. Then a glass for himself.

Haughtily she ignored hers.

"And I thought you were the girl with bad habits?"

She didn't smile, and he lit a cigarette.

"Those things are killing you," she whispered. "Every one you smoke takes seconds off your life."

He took another drag and expelled a perfect smoke ring. "Really? I'd think that would be a point in their favor as far as you're concerned."

She watched him—white-faced.

He downed his whiskey in a single draught.

"That's something else you shouldn't do."

"I do a lot of things I shouldn't," he muttered fiercely.

Her ashen face, her slanting green eyes watching him like a doe at bay—these things got to him.

Damn! He wanted to taste her again, but he knew one kiss wouldn't be enough. As if nothing extraordinary had happened between them, he pulled a chair out for her, and she sat down. He sprawled nonchalantly behind his desk.

"So where's Kirk?" Jeb demanded. He felt better after the cigarette and whiskey.

There was silence. She stared at him warily.

"You can take away all my licenses," she said quietly. "They mean nothing compared to Kirk's life."

"You're the hardest woman on earth to help, Megan. All I've ever tried to do is help you. That's all I want to do now."

"Really?" There was disbelief in her shaking tone.

"You're either the stupidest or the stubbornest woman alive. You've got no choice but to trust me, Megan. There's no one else."

She chewed her lip. "There's no way I can trust

you, but you're right about there not being a choice."
She stared at him for a long while. At last she sighed
in defeat. "Okay. You win. Don't you always?"

His mouth thinned. "Just tell me, Megan, without
the usual bunch of insults."

"Kirk's hurt. He may be dying. He's in Mexico
like you thought. So help me, Jeb, if you try to stop
me—"

"Just stick to the facts."

"A man called Dwight Creighton hired him to go
down there to get his wife and child. They had been
kidnapped and were being held for ransom."

"What's your part in all this?"

"Yesterday morning a man called me on the
phone. He said that the helicopter that was supposed
to get Kirk, the woman and the child out had been
shot down. He gave me the coordinates of an abandoned army strip in Mexico and told me to get there
at eight last night. I picked up the woman and child
and brought them back. But Kirk was too badly hurt
to be moved, and the Piper was overloaded as it was.
I barely cleared the treetops taking off. Jeb, I had to
leave him. If he dies…"

"Did you see him?"

"No, but the helicopter pilot is with him. I'm supposed to go back tonight for them."

"I'm going with you."

"Jeb, no! There's not enough room in my plane.
I'll be overloaded as it is!"

His mind was racing, making quick rough calculations. "We're taking the Mooney. It's faster. More dependable. We'll have radar. We'll get in and out before they even know we're there. Hell, the Mexican-American border is like a sieve, you know that. Surely one little plane can make it. I still can't believe you went down there alone in your Piper. That thing's hardly more than a toy."

Her brows flashed together. "I'll have you know my plane's no toy! With a landing speed of only thirty-eight knots I can put down almost anywhere. My landing gear's more dependable on a rough strip. Besides, four peoples' lives were at stake." She hesitated. "Jeb, there's a group of guerrilla bandits who'll shoot us if they catch us landing, unless we pay them an exorbitant landing fee. They're used to dealing with drug runners. They might shoot up your plane. You could get killed."

Jeb got up and came to Megan. "You really are blind to me, aren't you? How could we have grown up together, lived together, worked together for years, with you not knowing me at all? Kirk is like a big brother to me, and ever since Julia disappeared, I've always thought of you as a little sister. I'm not letting you go down there alone. You were crazy to do what you did last night. In fact, if things are as dangerous as you say, I don't want you going down there at all. You give me the location of that strip, and I'll get Tim Collins to fly me—"

"No."

"Megan, if they capture you... I don't like the thought of what they'd do to a woman."

She shuddered. "The answer's still no."

He remembered how obstinate she could be. He couldn't risk what she might try if he didn't agree. "Okay," he muttered softly. "You're going."

"Why are you so determined to go, Jeb?"

"Let's just say I'll be protecting the lives of the two best people on this ranch."

Megan blinked hard, her heart pounding fiercely. She remembered the passionate kiss they'd shared. "I've hated you for years."

"I know."

"But, in spite of everything, I feel better...just knowing you're coming with me. I never needed a friend more."

Jeb folded his large callused hand around hers possessively. "Then I guess it's a helluva thing to find yourself stuck with your worst enemy," he said with a slow grin.

"A helluva thing," she whispered, but instead of pulling her hand from his, she clung to it.

Four

___

Night rose in a thick, black smoke from the earth, making the valleys indistinguishable from the plains and hills. The occasional villages were lit up like constellations. Single houses were shining beacons lost in the inky vastness.

The Mooney was less than the tiniest pinprick in the eye of heaven.

Other than the roar of the engine, it was silent in the snug cockpit as Jeb and Megan scanned the darkness for any flares that would indicate the strip. They were deep over Mexico, flying low, with only the stars above, the lights beneath from the villages and the luminous dials on the instruments to guide them.

Megan felt the chill fingers of fear creep up and down her spine as she stared down into the yawning darkness and sensed the plane's terrible aloneness. Her eyes were glued to the dark earth. Dear God! It seemed she'd been in the plane for hours. Why weren't the flares down there? Her heart pounded in her throat. Did it mean Kirk was already dead?

She could feel Jeb's tension as he silently searched the darkness. He hated flying, almost more than he hated anything, and he was bound to be more nervous than usual tonight. In the bluish-gray glow of the instruments his hard features seemed etched from marble. How long would Jeb let her search before he made her give up?

Suddenly beneath them there were two rows of flickering lights.

Her heart lurched as she studied the angle of the strip. There was a nasty crosswind. The lights wobbled, and she realized raindrops had begun to splatter lightly against the windshield.

There was a jungle down there, dense, black and impenetrable. The thick night seemed to ooze up out of the mud.

She didn't like the rain. It would only make the short strip more dangerous.

She tried to concentrate on her instruments. But thoughts of drug runners and bandits and her wounded brother intruded. The flares could be a deadly trap.

She set up her approach.

What if someone had thrown a tree across the strip to wreck her plane? Men could be waiting down there to murder and rob them.

"Look down," she commanded, "and see if the strip's clear."

The plane buzzed the strip. The flares flickered brightly.

"Nothing," Jeb muttered.

"Okay," she whispered.

At eighty miles an hour they whistled down over the jungle.

The strip was short, too short for the Mooney, especially with the rain. She had to come in low over the trees, so close that the top branches brushed the belly of the plane.

One quick sideslip, and she lost the last of her altitude and made the final commitment to land on that short, black river between glimmering oil pots.

The trees were behind her. The flares rushed past in a frightening blur.

She was running out of runway.

For better or worse— She slammed the Mooney down into the sodden earth. The landing gear shot geysers of mud, slinging a storm of oozing dark liquid all over the plane.

Steering blind, Megan fought to keep the reeling plane in a straight path. One wheel jounced over something, and the Mooney slid to a stop. Her hand went to the master switch.

"Leave it on," Jeb whispered as he opened the door, "and stay near the plane." He jumped to the ground and held out his hand.

She stepped outside into the tropical heat and the shock of cool, crisping rain against her skin and clothes. The jungle was deep and dark, silently menacing as it encroached upon the strip. Despite the shower she could see stars.

A yellow beam bobbed in the trees and was gone. Two running figures loomed out of the darkness.

She saw the involuntary tightening of Jeb's hand on his gun.

"Don't," she whispered. "It's the helicopter pilot with the same Mexican he had with him last night."

"*Señorita*, your brother, he can't be moved. He said to leave him." This was the Mexican, breathless, his black eyes enormous with fear. She didn't trust him.

"Where's MacKay?" Jeb demanded.

"In a hut, *señor*, at the edge of the jungle."

"Take me to him."

"We can't, *señor*. The kidnappers are closing in. The bandits who charge a landing fee to all planes that use their strip, they come at any time." His black eyes darted to Megan. "If we don't go now, I cannot guarantee the lady will be all right."

Jeb slid the safety off his automatic. There was a

cool recklessness in his dark face. "I said take me to him." His voice was a deadly rasp. He jumped down onto the muddy strip.

"I'm going with you," Megan said, scampering after him.

The cool, silent rain soaked into her cotton shirt and jeans and ran in chilling rivulets down her hair. She began to shiver.

"Don't be crazy," Jeb muttered roughly, turning back to her, keeping his eyes on the other men as well.

"What if Kirk's dying?" Her voice shook. A single damp lock of hair fell over her brow. "W-what if I never get to see him again?"

She glanced fearfully toward Jeb and found no comfort in the ruthless set of his grim features. His black eyes were narrowed and so intense when they fell on her that they seemed to pierce through her, to the marrow of her soul. The rain had already soaked through his shirt, and the cloth was glued to his lean muscled body. He seemed dangerous, a stranger, not the man she knew at all.

Without a word he jammed the loaded forty-five he was holding into her hand. The metal felt hot from his grip. She watched him adjust his rifle to automatic fire. His voice came low and soft, and yet she heard it above the Mooney's engine. "Now is not the time for histrionics. Now is the time for gut-level decisions, and I'm going to make them. For once in your life, you'll do exactly as I say. Kirk's only chance and maybe *our* only chance is for me to go to him and for you to stay with the plane.''

''I'll never forgive you, never, if you're wrong. If he dies…''

Jeb snapped her roughly into his arms, knocking the breath from her lungs, and she was silent. The rest of her hair came undone and fell in a sodden plait down her back.

''So, what else is new?'' he whispered hoarsely. ''And, Megan, if those other guys, the ones after Kirk or the ones out to rob us, get here before we do, take off.''

Her head tilted back and she stared beseeching into his grim face. ''N-no. I—I couldn't leave you.''

A grin flitted briefly across his dark face and was gone. ''That's a switch,'' he murmured in a harsh, low tone, and yet his fingers were oddly gentle as he smoothed the wet hair out of her eyes.

''Please, Jeb, don't leave me.'' Megan was frantic as she tried to hold onto him. She felt the warmth and power of his arms through his ice-cold shirt.

To Jeb she seemed younger, more vulnerable. Even with the rain staining her clothes and making her fiery hair drip, she had never seemed softer, lovelier, more amazingly a woman—and most amazingly of all, his woman.

He felt a fierce melting at the quick. His grip tightened on her arms. "Honey," he muttered savagely, "I'm coming back."

She felt his fingers dig into the flesh of her upper arms.

"I'm too ornery to die, when I've just found out I want you as badly as I do."

Her arms slid around his powerful neck, across his back, drawing him closer. He bent his head, searched for her mouth and found it. He kissed her warm lips roughly, quickly, and she kissed him back. She was part of the darkness, part of the black fluid heat of all his memories and tangled desires.

He buried his mouth in her hair and tasted the tantalizing sweetness of wild roses as well as the fresh flavor of the rain. His arms were around her, pressing her into his body. Her own arms were locked just as tightly around his broad shoulders. He felt the dizzy vertigo of his endless, aching need. How many years had he longed for this and yet denied her power over him?

His lips devoured hers hungrily.

"Hold me," she whispered brokenly, "just hold me."

He let her go. For an instant she clung even tighter, her eyes seeking his in the darkness. Then knowing she could never hold him against his will, she let her hands fall away.

Because he was leaving her she felt cold and empty, depleted, afraid of the blackness, of this night, afraid as she'd never been afraid. Because he was leaving her.

"If I'm not back in half an hour, go," he commanded.

An agony as profound as his own was in her enormous bleak eyes.

She shook her head silently and held out her trembling hand to him.

"Listen to me, you little fool. If I can't make it back here, our only chance will be for you to get out and get help."

Her hands flew to her lips. She choked back a sob.

"Promise me," he growled, "or I swear, if we live, you'll regret it."

If...

For Megan there was only the incessant sewing-machine-like roar of the prop. Only the pelt of the bone-chilling rain. Only Jeb leaving her.

She rallied briefly. "Who do you think you are, Jeb Jackson, a king?"

"Damn right." But his voice went soft. "Promise me, so I can get the hell out of here and save Kirk."

The threat was silky smooth, but for all its softness, it was still a threat. At last she nodded forlornly. She closed her eyes, unable to watch him go.

He turned toward the men. "Okay. Take me to him."

"*Si, señor.*"

When she opened her eyes she was alone.

She stared into the dark jungle, wishing she had watched him walk away, wishing she knew exactly what spot of that dense growth had swallowed him, wondering why the mere thought of him in danger was tearing out her soul.

She had hated him for years. No woman with a grain of sense could endure such a man. He was spoiled, selfish, insolent, pigheaded, demanding—in short, impossible.

Tonight he had been no different. He had treated her arrogantly, high-handedly ordering her about as he always did, commanding her to stay with the plane as though she were his lackey, keeping her from Kirk, who might be dying. And yet, now that Jeb was gone, it seemed he was her dearest, most trusted friend, that he alone could be depended on to keep her safe. It came as a startling surprise to realize how much delightful enjoyment she had taken in hating him.

What if he didn't come back? What if she never saw him again?

Megan felt a swift stab of black, all-engulfing loneliness. What if she never again knew the piercing thrill of his hard lips taking hers?

She could still taste the flavor of his mouth. She could still remember the way every muscle in his body had gone tight with desire when he held her.

Tears swam in her eyes.

She sucked in her breath sharply. She would go crazy if she kept thinking about it.

The pilot in her took over. She checked the plane for any damage that might have resulted from the rough landing. Luckily there was none. She cleaned the windshield. She got inside and maneuvered the plane so it was positioned for takeoff. Then she paced the runway in front of the Mooney, moving blown branches and occasional stones, trying to memorize where all the potholes were. The further she moved away from the plane, the fainter the whir of the engine became.

The strip seemed deserted, but she realized someone could be watching her. Someone could dash to the plane and take off and be gone. She ran back to the Mooney to wait.

The darkness and the waiting were unendurable. A mist was rising from the damp earth on all sides of the strip. The cloud-choked glow of a golden moon rose above the trees, and the jungle seemed to glisten.

The drizzle changed to a violent downpour. If the rain kept up, the strip would soon be unusable.

There was the crackle of distant thunder. A flash of light.

Above, through a thin patch of cloud, she could still see stars.

The rain pounded against the wings of the plane. Her eyes strained in the darkness. Oh, where was Jeb?

She glanced at her watch and realized with horror that he'd been gone longer than half an hour.

A nightmarish haze of panic gripped her. Jeb had commanded her to leave.

She studied the minute hand of her watch as it made two lazy rotations around the dial. The rain continued to swirl down in sheets.

She heard the thunder again and saw the flickers of light. A bullet ricocheted off a tree trunk.

It was gunfire, not thunder!

The next bullet erupted two feet in front of her, slinging mud onto her jeans.

Someone was shooting at her!

She inched toward the plane and crawled inside.

Bullets sprayed wildly from the jungle, but not in her direction.

Then there was an awful silence.

She held her breath.

Three stooped figures emerged from the trees. They were running, crouching low, carrying something heavy.

In the rain it was impossible to recognize them. She squinted, sick with the agony of not knowing.

Her hand was on the throttle. Then she removed it, knowing that if she guessed wrong, it would mean her life.

Horrible visions of rape and torture preceding her murder flashed through her mind. Gulping a deep breath, she threw open the door.

It was Jeb and the men, carrying Kirk on a makeshift stretcher.

Behind them she could hear the staccato bursts of more gunfire.

Jeb threw himself on the ground and fired in rapid succession toward the jungle to cover the other men as they hauled Kirk into the cockpit.

Even in the darkness Megan could see Kirk was desperately hurt. She took his hand, and beneath the thick silver bracelet he always wore, his pulse made only the faintest throb against her fingertip. When she released his wrist, it fell limply to his side. She brushed his hair away from his forehead and murmured his name, but he did not answer.

He was burning hot. Beneath the black streaks on his face, his skin was ashen. It pained her to see her tough, powerfully rugged brother so silent, so defenseless. Blood seeped through a crude, dirty bandage wound around his head. His camouflage pants were slashed from cuff to knee, and around his calf another filthy bandage was dark with blood. His eyes were closed. His almost girlishly long lashes lay in inky fringes against his bloodless cheeks. He was so thin and battered-looking. She was almost glad that he was unconscious.

Men streamed out of the jungle to block the runway just as Jeb jumped inside the plane, blood pouring down the side of his face.

"Dear God," she moaned, reaching out to touch him, forgetting the small army rushing toward them.

"It's nothing," Jeb growled, "just a scratch. Fly the damn plane."

The men knelt to take aim.

"Are they the guys after Kirk or the ones in control of the strip?" Megan asked.

"Who the hell cares!" Jeb thundered. "Take off, Megan."

"But they're down there, on the runway. I might hit one of them!"

He swore viciously. "Women! I knew I should have had Tim fly us instead of you."

Jeb always knew exactly what to say to get to her.

Stung, she headed the plane straight toward the firing men. Several bullets hit the wings and fuselage. All the lights on the panel went out.

She couldn't see her instruments. There was no way of knowing if the fuselage or anything else was damaged as the heavy wheels rolled forward, ever faster, jouncing over rocky ground.

Mud splashed the windshield in wide-arched rooster tails. She saw brown faces, brief, cruel images of white-eyed, evil men, throwing their guns to the ground and scattering out of the way. Mud spattered from the wheels of the racing plane, then sprayed hard in all directions. In an instant the Mooney was skimming above the grass, heading for the wall of trees at the end of the strip.

The wall loomed nearer. In the rain the strip was

too short. They were hurtling toward the trees at one-hundred-and-sixty miles an hour.

Every nerve in Megan's body froze. They weren't going to make it!

Jeb shielded his eyes with his hands, and she thought she heard him praying.

Megan watched in horror as trees rushed up to meet them. At the last second she thought she saw a small pocket in the wall, and she aimed for it. Two tall trees, a wingspan apart, loomed near. But at the last second Megan pulled the yoke back hard and made a steep climbing turn.

Fluttering leaves brushed by them. Miraculously they were above the trees, leaving them smooth and untouched, casting down a shuddering black shadow.

The rain had slackened. The moon was blazing.

Slowly Jeb dared to remove his hands from his eyes. In the moonlight his bloody face was as white as a sheet of poster board daubed with vivid red paint.

The instrument panel was still dark, and she began to jiggle several knobs. Jeb slammed his fist against the panel. "Come on! Damn you!"

"That's no way to treat sophisticated equipment," Megan muttered glumly.

He banged the panel again.

The lights flickered a couple of times and then came back on. The silent radio exploded into life.

Jeb's brows lifted cockily. "Well, it worked," he replied. His lips twitched in a faint, triumphant smile, indicating male superiority. "Even you can't argue with that." Before she could think of an adequate retort, he issued a battery of fresh orders. "Head for the Gulf. I want you to make contact with an airline pilot the minute you're over open water. We need to establish a flight plan as soon as we can so that this flight will look as normal as possible."

Numbly she obeyed. It was in his nature to command.

Even when she was flying.

She forced herself to remember it was his airplane.

Soon they were over the Gulf with the night sky enveloping them like a shimmering veil of gossamer. Megan tried not to think about Kirk, lying unconscious behind her. She tried not to think that if the damaged plane went down over the water, there was not even the faintest possibility they would survive. She concentrated on flying, and she flew the Mooney as though it were a part of her, piloting with her heart and soul, as well as her brain.

Near the outskirts of Brownsville, Texas, she landed the plane on a private strip that belonged to a rancher Jeb knew. Megan had radioed ahead for an ambulance, and it rushed toward the plane the minute she rolled it to a stop just short of the hangar.

Then they were in the ambulance, screaming toward the hospital, down endless palm-lined roads.

The smell of antiseptic nauseated Megan. It was the odor of illness and terrible injury, the cloyingly heavy scent of death. The pale green walls of the tiny waiting room seemed to close in on her like prison bars. She was suffocating.

If only it could be she who was dying, instead of Kirk.

In her right hand she clutched Kirk's silver bracelet with the wolfhound engraved on its face as if it were a talisman, squeezing the thick silver links until they bit into her flesh. Kirk had been in surgery for hours. His life hung by a spider's thread. He'd been shot twice and lost a lot of blood. He was feverish and his wounds were infected. The doctors had said there was little hope. Jeb and the doctors had clashed briefly when they'd asked him too many questions.

Jeb sat across the room, smoking, but this once, the habit did not bother her. She was too thankful for his strong, silent presence.

There was a white strip of medical tape along the side of his face where a bullet had grazed him. Jeb put out the cigarette and rose slowly to his feet. "This could go on a lot longer. I think I'll go get us both a cup of coffee."

"You know I don't drink coffee."

"You will tonight."

"Jeb…"

His mouth twisted. "They don't have herbal tea in the machine. Only Cokes and candy and coffee and all sorts of other unhealthy junk foods."

She shrugged, too exhausted to argue.

When he came back, she took the cup meekly from him. The coffee was hot and strong. It tasted better than she'd ever dreamed it could, warming her somehow, making her feel less tired.

When she was finished, he took her hand and pulled her onto the couch beside him, placing her bright head against his shoulder.

"Shut your eyes," he commanded gently.

"Kirk…"

"No news means he's alive."

Still she struggled, but Jeb wouldn't let her go.

"Shut your eyes," he said again pressing her close to him.

"I can't stop worrying," she murmured against his chest.

"Neither can I."

Somehow those words were a comfort.

Megan fell asleep in his arms, whether for hours or for minutes, she couldn't tell. But when she awoke, she felt better.

Sleep had loosened her inhibitions, and she'd put her hands where they didn't belong. She jumped away from him quickly, as if burned, realizing what she'd done as she withdrew her hot fingers from between his thighs.

She rose stiffly, ashamed of the intimacy she had subconsciously sought with him. "How long was I—?"

"Not long."

She felt the quick heat ebb from her cheeks, leaving her cold and pale. "I—I'm sorry."

"There's no need to be." Something smoldered dangerously in his eyes.

Megan's gaze remained fixed on his rugged face, and the burning color washed back into her cheeks. There was knowledge in his eyes.

"I didn't mean…to touch you…there," she stammered.

Another of his quick glances swept over her. "I know."

He got up, too, and stretched. He seemed huge in the little room. Hungrily she watched the fabric of his shirt play over muscle.

He came to her and brushed her cheek gently with his hand. "Will you be all right if I go out for a few minutes and make a couple of calls? I want to phone the ranch and have one of the hands drive a car down here with some clothes, and with Tim Collins. I want Tim to fly the Mooney back to the ranch before anyone gets too interested in those bullet holes. And I promised Janelle I'd call her. I'll be right outside if you need me."

"Of course, I'll be all right," Megan said, struggling to pretend she didn't mind.

Jeb hesitated, seeing the vulnerability in her eyes.

"Go on!" Megan whispered.

When he returned, he found her huddled hollow-eyed in a corner.

"Still no word?" he murmured.

She stirred restlessly and shook her head.

He sat down beside her and took her hand in his. "He'll make it," Jeb whispered. "Kirk's like you. He's too cussed stubborn to let a couple of Mexican bullets be the end of him."

Rough calluses ran caressingly against the soft flesh of her palm.

Megan sat there, smiling wanly, watching as Jeb's large brown hand slid against her golden one, liking the way his rough, cool fingers felt against her hot ones. "I imagine you're right," she said at last, "about us being stubborn."

"I know I am."

"Thanks."

"It wasn't a compliment," he murmured, "calling you cussed and stubborn."

"I was being sarcastic."

He smiled. "Just making sure."

"You never miss an opportunity to insult me."

"You'd be surprised." There was a hint of cynicism in his expression. "I rein in a few."

"If Kirk lives... Jeb, I'll be grateful to you forever."

Jeb smiled. He let go of her hand. She felt his fingers brush the flowing flame of tangled hair beside her face. Her heart fluttered, and she swallowed a soft moan.

"I always wondered what it would take to make you grateful." His fingers twirled a lock of her hair. "I would have thrown Kirk in the lion's den years ago and plucked him out again, if only I'd known. But I didn't. You know, Megan, through the years I thought I'd tried everything. Like I said, you MacKays are a stubborn lot. You, in particular. You can hold onto a grudge more tenaciously than any woman alive. I wonder—are all your emotions equally tenacious?"

His electric black gaze jolted through her. His hand kept curling the flyaway tendrils beside her cheek. For a numbed moment, she could only stare at the thick raven lock that tumbled carelessly across his forehead, at the black brows that made slashing arches above his brilliant black eyes. His features seemed roughly chiseled, harder somehow than mere flesh and bone, yet gentle.

She knew too well that he was a man who took what he wanted, a man who let nothing stand in his way. Hadn't he taken her ranch, humiliated and driven her father away? Her gratitude toward Jeb dissolved in the hot tide of bitterness that filled her.

She recoiled from him. "I had good reason to hate you," she whispered.

She tried to move away, but he wouldn't let her.

"You thought you had good reason." His voice was as bitter as hers.

They stared at one another for a long time. "If Kirk lives, he's got to get over this obsession about rescuing people," she said, struggling to change the subject.

"He's not going to," Jeb replied matter-of-factly. "He can't stop blaming himself for what happened to Julia. He wasn't tough enough to stop them from taking her, so he went into the Marines and later the CIA to make himself tough enough. Kirk made himself into a lethal weapon. I think that's why he can't say no to people when they come to him with a problem. Every time he goes into some country to help somebody in trouble, he's saving Julia."

"Maybe after this he'll be different."

"Get smart, Megan! Kirk won't change! No matter how many people he rescues, he can't save Julia, so he'll keep on going…until…his luck runs out—" Jeb finished darkly.

"No." The single word was a moan of pain. "If he lives, I'm not going to let him risk his life like this again! If… That's the key word, isn't it? Oh, Jeb, if Kirk dies, I'll be all alone."

Jeb folded her into his arms. "Honey, you've never been alone. You've always had me and my family behind you. You were just too proud to see it."

An uncontrollable shiver raced down her spine at his nearness.

She didn't want to let him hold her, but his warmth seeped inside her seductively. She sagged weakly in the arms of the man she'd hated for years, in the arms of the man who'd stolen everything she valued.

But he had risked his life to save her brother, and for that she owed him.

Megan's eyes flew to Jeb's face. His expression was hard, implacable.

The intense emotions he aroused in her were bewildering. She didn't know anymore if he was friend or foe.

She only knew she was irresistibly drawn to him, and she was terribly afraid it would prove a fatal fascination.

Five

There was a crackle of sound in the room as the miniblinds were flicked open. A blood red sun splashed ribs of fire from a high, narrow window into the cold room that reeked faintly of stale cigarettes. Megan snapped herself up sharply from the comforting warmth of Jeb's arms.

The first thing she saw was the doctor in his blue scrub suit, and her heart began to thrum with terror for her brother.

The doctor's mask hung limply around his neck. His face was gray and lined from the hours in the operating room. His bloodshot blue eyes were large with the same frank curiosity he'd had last night when they had showed up in his emergency room. They'd been in blood-soaked clothes with a dying man who looked like a mercenary soldier shot full of bullet holes.

The doctor had thrown off Kirk's sheet, looked at him with those cold, curious eyes and demanded rudely, "Mind telling me about it, sir?"

"Yes!" Jeb had erupted. "You're wasting precious time—time he doesn't have."

Filthy and mud-caked, his brown face crusted with blood and his black eyes burning, Jeb had looked ferocious.

"I can't operate until I know."

Jeb had loomed over the smaller man. "You can do anything you damn well decide to do. I'm Jeb Jackson of Jackson Ranch."

"Nobody's above the law."

"I didn't say I was. That man on the stretcher works for me. I don't know what happened to him for sure. I just found him. If you can't save him, find someone who can. I'm known as a man who repays favors, and I'll consider it a favor if Kirk MacKay lives."

Megan had listened in numb silence. The doctor hesitated. All Megan could see was Kirk lying between them, his tanned face ashen, the lifeblood seeping out of him.

"For God's sake, save my brother," Megan had cried.

The doctor had stared at her for a long moment. Then he'd picked up the phone and dialed an administrator. After that call there were no more questions. Only brisk, tight-lipped efficiency.

Megan had always despised Jeb's tactics. They were low-down and undemocratic, exactly like him, but this time it was gratifying to see how well they worked. Within minutes a team of surgeons had begun working to save Kirk. A second standby team was flown in from Harlingen.

In the red morning sunlight, the doctor studied Megan.

"I-is Kirk dead?" Her voice was choked with fear.

Jeb woke up instantly, and the doctor's expression hardened.

"He's going to make it."

"You must have operated all night."

"What was left of it, yes, but your brother's tough. Wounds such as he sustained would have killed most men. His knowledge of first aid plus his other survival skills must have enabled him to hold on until you found him and brought him here. Of course, especially for the next twenty-four hours, there's always the chance of complications."

"Can we see MacKay?" Jeb asked.

"He's unconscious."

Jeb scowled blackly at him.

"Just for a minute," the doctor said.

It was a comfort to Megan to see Kirk's white face

even for the brief half minute the doctor allowed them, to hold his still hand. It was a comfort to see that he really had survived the long hours on the operating table.

"Kirk," she whispered, "you made it. You're going to be okay." Her finger traced the curve of his thumb.

Jeb led her gently outside. "He can't hear you."

"I just wanted him to know."

"He knows."

They came out of the recovery room. She started to sink onto the couch, but Jeb restrained her, shaking his dark head. "No, I'm taking you to a motel, where you can stretch out comfortably."

"I'm not leaving Kirk."

Dark eyes moved over her face. "The motel's only five minutes away. I made the reservation last night when I used the phone."

"You were that sure he'd make it?"

"I told you he was too stubborn to die."

"And I'm too stubborn to go to a motel room with you."

Jeb gave her a long look and shrugged indifferently. "Then stay here alone, if that's what you want."

She watched him pick up his things. She listened to him give the nurse his phone number.

At the door, he turned. "Well," came his quiet low

tone. "If you need anything, the nurse knows where I'll be."

Megan cocked her head in a defiant angle, but her soft voice was not so defiant. "You say it's only five minutes away?"

"Maybe less," he murmured.

The throbbing of her pulse echoed loudly in her ears. "I—I hate being by myself."

"I know the feeling." His voice was husky.

Both of them were silent again.

The ribbons of light were now golden against the wall. He didn't move, and they couldn't stop looking at each other. His bronzed face was dark, unfathomable.

They both spoke at once.

"Megan…"

"Jeb…"

Their names were soft sounds, cutting into the silence, then vanishing.

Across the stillness they laughed nervously.

His mouth crooked into a charming half smile. "You coming or not?" he asked huskily.

She shook her head, but when he opened the door, she jumped up with her purse and ran after him.

He turned. In the gleaming white hall, wearing his bloodied camouflage fatigues, he seemed an all-powerful male giant. The rugged planes of his face, tanned by the sun and made darker by the jet blackness of his eyes and hair increased the pagan force that drew her to him. His brooding gaze moved possessively across her face, and she knew a moment's alarm.

She had made a mistake. He exuded masculine power and virility. No woman in her right mind would go to a motel room alone with such a man unless she was willing to...

His black gaze seared her, and Megan began to shiver. She was exhausted. She didn't want to be alone; that was all. He held out his hand, and with an exaggerated show of reluctance, she placed her own in it.

He smiled down at her, a triumphant gleam in his eyes. His grip was like hot living steel. "If I'd forced you," he chuckled softly, "you would have fought me all the way. Maybe I'm learning how to handle you."

The last sentence should have been a warning.

But she could not resist the effect his gentleness had on her senses. He brought her fingers to his lips and kissed them tenderly, and she made no attempt to pull away.

Megan had second thoughts as she stood outside the motel room and watched Jeb turn the key. He led her inside.

An immense red-satin, king-size bed gleamed from the center of the room.

"Looks good, doesn't it?" Jeb drawled with a lazy smile.

There was an unreal quality about the moment, a terrifying magic that set her senses spinning. Her legs turned to jelly. Red satin blurred into a shimmering scarlet sea that seemed to fill the room.

"I-isn't there another room? Or at least another bed?" Megan asked in a tiny, shaking voice.

"This is it," he murmured. "The last bed in Brownsville. Take it or leave it."

"I'm leaving," she whispered, her heart racing in panic. She made a wild jump toward the door.

"Don't be silly." He caught her at the door, peeled her fingers from the door facing and brought her back inside. At his touch a liquid fire raced through her senses.

"I really don't think..." She whirled, and he wrapped her tightly in his taut arms.

"You're behaving like a child. Do you really think I brought you here to seduce you?" He laughed softly when her eyes filled guiltily with telling emotion. "Believe me, until you started acting like this, that was the last thing on my mind. I'm tired and filthy and so are you. Every time that doctor looks at us, he acts like we're criminals. I want a bath and an hour's sleep."

"I'd still rather go back to the hospital," she insisted mulishly.

"Look, nothing's going to happen." His lips

curved. "Unless you do something to make it happen."

Green eyes flashed. "I'm certainly not going to do anything!"

"Well, there you have it. You're safer with me than if you were in a convent."

She stared into his ruggedly handsome face. "Safer?" Her eyes trailed over the rippling expanse of his muscled shoulders in startled disbelief.

He grinned. "You have me to protect you."

"What about those kisses?" she blurted. Megan felt heat flush her face.

His eyes traced the curve of her vivid, lush lips.

"What about them?" he demanded softly.

"Yesterday morning, and…" She watched the telltale pulse tick within the corded column of his neck, belying his air of lazy nonchalance. "You're so big. You could make me do anything you wanted," she said, trying to still the quiver in her voice.

"This is now, and in case you've forgotten, we've both just been through hell. I've never forced myself on a woman."

She lifted her chin. "You're saying you don't think anything of sharing a room and a bed with me."

"It damn well beats sharing that plastic couch in that ice-cold waiting room."

She resented the twisted logic in that statement.

"Don't look so worried. I'm the guy that didn't make a move even when you invited me into your bedroom and offered yourself to me." His dark head was thrown back, and he was staring arrogantly down at her.

She flushed. "You're never going to let me forget that, are you?"

"It's a cherished memory." He smiled sensually, maddeningly.

"If you were a gentleman…"

"We both know I'm not." He flashed her another of his quick white smiles.

"That fact is hardly reassuring."

He laughed boldly. His hands ran down the length of her arms while a compelling light glittered in his eyes. "I'm beginning to think it's not me you don't trust, but yourself, honey."

She swallowed, digesting this new thought. The fact that there was some truth to his brash statement was even less reassuring.

He stalked away and began to unbutton his shirt. As he did, her eyes widened and she stared at the teak-brown strip of his chest. The curling mat of hair on the broad expanse ran down the center of him, tapering to a line at the waistband of his trousers. He stopped, aware of her mesmerized stare, and nodded toward her.

"Sorry. I'm so used to living alone, I forgot." A thick black brow arched sardonically. "Ladies first."

The bed was between them, making her more

deeply conscious of being in a bedroom, alone with him.

Megan gazed helplessly into his dark face. "W-what?" she stammered.

"Your clothes are smeared with Kirk's blood. You need a bath."

Her face flamed. "I'm not taking my clothes off."

"Suit yourself."

He stripped down to his trousers. When he fumbled with his zipper, she clamped her eyelids tightly shut.

He laughed with amusement as though he derived great entertainment from her modesty. She heard him move with deadly, pantherlike agility toward the bathroom.

"You can open your eyes now," he said, shutting the door with a soft click, still chuckling to himself.

Megan sat rigidly on the bed, listening to him in the bathroom. There were the sounds of soap wrappers being torn off and discarded, of water splashing, of a low velvet rumble as he sang bawdily to himself.

He was perfectly at ease. He was probably enjoying himself immensely. Minutes later the bathroom door opened again. A delicious, male-scented cloud of steam preceded him. She jumped off the bed.

He stood before her, his body sleek and brown, his face bright, his hair as wet as jet ink. He smiled jauntily into her worried face. A damp sheen clung to his body. He smelled of soap. Other pleasant scents wafted toward her. Jeb took a deep breath as if the air were keener now that he was clean. He seemed to feel invigorated, but she almost preferred him dirty and tired—not so vitally energetic.

He wore nothing but a towel as he strutted about the room without showing the least concern that it might fall off. She found herself marveling at him. His body was all muscle, even his flat, hard stomach. Hungrily she studied the dark trail of fur that ran from his chest down to the towel. Some treacherous part of her began almost to wish that the towel would fall off so she could find out if the hidden parts of him were as dark and virilely attractive as the rest. She flushed and stole a quick glance at his face to see if he might have read her thoughts, but he wasn't watching her. He didn't seem in the least bothered by her avid interest. She shook her head, but the magic of being alone with him was beginning to work its spell on her.

He rubbed his roughened chin. "I wish I had a razor."

She wished he did, too. The dark shadow against his cheek and jaw only served to make him seem more virile.

"You can have the bathroom now," he said. When she clung to the bed, frozen, he murmured dryly, "And I always thought females were the fastidious sex."

He moved toward her. At the last minute, before he reached her, she scampered lightly past him and slammed the door, having decided to bathe only to avoid being alone with him in the bedroom.

She lathered her hair. He had switched on the television while he waited for her. Stubbornly she lay in the hot soapy water until it grew cool, until no sound came from the other room. When at last she crept from the bath to the bedroom wearing a thin robe supplied by the motel staff, she stood in the center of it, feeling lost and uncertain, shivering a little from the cold as she studied the black shapes in the darkened room.

He was in bed with the covers pulled to his waist. His eyes were closed. He could have been asleep, but he was such a devil he was probably only pretending to be. His towel was draped over the chair near the bed.

What did he have on? The only way to know for sure was to rip his cover off or wake him up to ask him.

"Jeb?"

Blasts of frigid air gusted noisily from the air conditioner, and she began to shiver. With her wet hair, she couldn't very well stand in the middle of the room shivering until he woke up. She tiptoed toward the bed and lifted the spread on her side of the bed. Gingerly she slipped her legs under the sheets.

His deep voice rumbled across the darkness.

"Good night, Megan."

So he had been awake!

She lay as rigidly as a post, not answering.

He grunted, rolled over and made some sound as he adjusted himself beneath the rustling sheets. She felt the mattress dip as he shifted his weight. Beside him, she was a tense ball of nerves, afraid to move, ready to spring from the bed if he made the slightest move toward her.

Soon she heard the steady rhythm of his breathing. He had fallen asleep. Instantly. As if her presence in his bed didn't bother him in the least.

She lay awake, too aware of his clean male scent, too aware of that indolent brown sprawl of muscled arms and legs so near her own beneath the covers. At his slightest movement, she caught her breath.

Oddly, after a time, his nearness was a comfort, and at last she relaxed and fell asleep, too, though she clung to her edge of the mattress.

Almost immediately the recurring nightmare she'd had ever since she was five and her mother had run away began.

Megan was in an oak mott, and she, who'd grown up on the wide-open range beneath endless blue skies, was afraid of the thick, gnarled trees with their dark branches that shut out the sun. She was alone. Her family, which had been with her only moments before, had dissolved into the silent, terrifying aloneness.

She began to run, but no matter where she turned, she could not find them.

"Here," a voice murmured, and she felt the warm comfort of hard male arms circling her breathless body, holding her close.

She felt safe, no longer alone, and she snuggled against him, seeking the delicious warmth of his body, nestling her head into the hollow of his throat, wrapping her arms around him, exploring the ripple of his muscles with her fingertips. Never before had her dream taken this pleasant turn.

A bare masculine arm encircled her waist; warm breathing ruffled the hair at her temple. A sigh of pleasure escaped her lips as she was drawn closer and pressed into a rock-hard chest. Curling black hairs tickled her nose and she sighed blissfully. Closer still, he pulled her, cuddling her hips against his own. He was naked. She felt his manhood, like a branding pulse, fully roused against her thighs.

As her flesh heated against his, she came awake gradually, not admitting it in the magic of that first drowsily sensual moment, clinging to the fantasy until it was too late.

"Megan," he murmured.

It was Jeb holding her, Jeb whom she'd both loved and hated through the years. Jeb who'd always been there. Jeb who'd risked his own life to save her brother.

She could feel the deep thrust of Jeb's satirical gaze piercing the darkness, studying her. In that moment he would have stopped had she asked him to.

But how many times had she awakened, crying in the dark, with no one to hold her? How many times had she dreamed of this? It was too delicious, being held and comforted by him.

Sighing, she snuggled closer to him. There was more wildness in her than in most other women, a deep, innate sensuality. Her body burned a degree hotter than usual. She met his intense gaze with a brief, silent glance.

He put one hand on either side of her hot cheeks and turned her face slowly toward his in wonder. Her eyes fluttered open right before he took her mouth with silent, masterful deliberateness, kissing her again and again. His tongue slid inside her mouth. Her breath came shallowly as her own tongue flicked against his.

His lips slid down her throat, over her body, kissing her everywhere, seeking out all the soft secret places, until she arched her body against his exploring mouth.

He was darkness and she was darkness, both like figments from her volatile dream, and yet not a dream at all. His mouth came back to her lips. He devoured them, suckled them. She could feel her skin burning, everywhere, from the bristles of his beard, but she welcomed even this tingling awareness of him.

They kissed and touched until they were consumed in a delirium of passion. Vaguely she knew that it was Jeb who held her, that what was happening was wrong, and yet she knew that there was nothing on earth that could make her stop.

He tore the robe off her completely and pulled her beneath his hard body.

"You'll belong to me after this," he said ruthlessly. "Forever."

Her hands circled his neck. She was past caring. "Forever," she promised, her cheeks flushed, her eyes brilliant and daring.

"There won't be any going back."

"No... Don't ever...ever let me go...."

"Touch me," he growled. "Hold me."

She closed her fingers around him, and she felt his pulsating, driving desire.

"Tighter!" he said.

She gasped when his hand closed over hers, pulling her fingers away, easing her thighs apart.

He came inside her at once, and she knew that she had always belonged to him. Her fingernails dug into his neck, and yet, curiously, she did not hurt him. For both of them there was only a sublime, shattering joy.

She screamed and every cell in her body exploded.

Afterward Megan lay in the semidarkness feeling lost and vulnerable and thoroughly shaken. Jeb's knee remained crooked over her legs. A possessive brown hand rested indolently on her waist. She wanted to pull away, but she didn't dare. He would only come after her and demand that she explain herself. And she didn't want to.

Her emotions were too new, too raw and agonized. All her life she had longed for love and denied her longing. She had pretended to be proud and tough and independent. She had pretended to hate Jeb long after the hate had died because it was so much easier to hate than to love and be abandoned again.

She had longed to feel safe and wanted—the way Jeb had made her feel in those brief, shining moments when he'd held her tightly clasped in his arms and made love to her.

Being with him had been wonderful, something totally outside her experience.

That was what made it so terrible.

Even though he had saved Kirk, and she was grateful, Jeb had taken her ranch and driven her father away. Worst of all, Jeb belonged to Janelle.

Megan's heart beat with dull little thuds.

He had taken her because it was in his nature to rule and dominate. He had to be king of everything he thought belonged to him.

Jeb was not Megan's first lover, but he might as well have been. Never had any man branded her heart and soul as thoroughly as he had.

But she was nothing to him, and it was killing her. She was only a bit of temporary fun before he settled down with someone more suitable—someone like Janelle.

Across the tense, silent darkness Jeb reached for her. She could feel his hand as he idly traced his knuckles over her ribs and smoothed a lock of apricot hair on her shoulder.

"You said you wouldn't," she accused angrily.

"You said you wouldn't," he mimicked in an exaggerated version of her horrified tone. He chuckled. "Well, I'm not mad at *you* for what happened."

"You're not a woman!"

Again he chuckled. "We'd hardly be lying here like this if I were."

"You're going to marry Janelle."

"But I'm in bed with you." His fingertip brushed her cheek. "Not Janelle."

"Don't rub it in!" Megan bit her lower lip. Her lashes were downcast. "What happened doesn't have to mean anything. Things can go on between us…like they were before."

His eyes grew bleak and cold in the darkness. She could feel the tension in his fingers, tracing soft patterns on her hot skin.

"Things between us can never be like they were before," he said grimly.

He wound his hand in the waves of her fiery hair and pulled her close to him. His mouth crushed down on hers.

"Because I still want you," he whispered raggedly against her cheek. "And you still want me."

Every muscle in Megan's body was tensed against

him, but her strength was as nothing to his. With his hands he guided her breasts to his mouth, seeking out her nipples and nibbling on them until her tension erupted into unbearable excitement. Her fingers gripped his shoulders tightly, and she pulled his head closer against her burning skin, crying out as he suckled the hot, fleshy tips.

"All your life you've wanted this," he whispered. "You've wanted me, and you've wanted to belong to me."

"No."

He lifted his head. "Yes!" he whispered.

Breathless for him, she tried to push his lips back down to her tingling flesh.

"Say yes!" he commanded her. His black eyes were as hard and cold as diamonds as he studied her face.

Her expression altered slightly, mirroring some subtle change of emotion. Megan was afraid. Not of him, but of herself.

"Say it."

"Y-yes." The word fell hesitantly, softly from her lips.

Suddenly he wanted to stroke her cheek and tell her that the spell she'd cast over him was more powerful than any hold he could ever have on her. There was something wondrous about her beauty and about the emotion it aroused in him. It was closer to worship than lust.

He lowered his mouth and tasted her again until she was clinging and biting her lips to suppress her cries, until she could no longer suppress them.

There was only the ecstasy of his hot body, only her soft, keening cries of rapture.

There could be no denying that she was his.

Six

Sunlight flickered across Megan's soft pink nipples.
She felt the sun's heat and stirred lazily. Then her big
toe struck the warmth of hard thigh muscle.

"Ouch!" came a surprised male yelp.

The danger of the man standing beside the bed
seeped gradually into Megan's consciousness.

Jeb had opened the drapes, and harsh, midmorning
sunshine flooded into the room from behind him.
Slowly her gaze focused on his broad-shouldered figure, her eyes widening with instinctive fear. Elegantly
dressed, he sat down on the edge of the bed beside
her, his dark face shadowed, his gaze intent.

The shock of what had happened last night came

back to Megan in a flash. Bright flags of color stained her cheeks. Her heart fluttered warily. Jeb was dressed in a three-piece suit and tie. Mario must have come and brought fresh clothes. Jeb seemed so cool this morning, so controlled, so cockily self-assured.

Realizing with a start that her nude body was uncovered beneath his avid gaze, Megan felt vulnerable and exposed. There was no way of knowing how long he had been watching her and enjoying her provocative position. As if it were his right to look at her like that, with a possessive gleam of ownership in his eyes!

Her shining hair was spread across the pillow like a web of fire. He leaned forward and gently brushed a finger through it.

She jerked her head away, but a russet strand snagged around his thumb. His eyes glinted as they ran over her. Flushing scarlet, she drew her legs together and snatched a sheet over her breasts.

He chuckled. "I'd say it's a little late for modesty between us."

He pulled at the sheet, but she held on to it with equal stubbornness. "What do you think you're doing?" she gasped.

"Trying to enjoy the best view in town," he murmured.

"Any man with an ounce of decency..."

"Since we both know your low opinion of me, you

must be addressing someone else." With devilish delight he kept pulling.

"Jeb, please!"

Her face flamed as the edge of the sheet slid down to her waist. He let go. She felt ridiculously awkward and out of her depth. "I want to get dressed."

His lips quirked with amusement. "What a pity."

"You'll have to get up and go outside. Or at least close your eyes," she said.

"But I saw it all last night—at a much closer and more delightful range." He smiled wickedly.

Her throat constricted. She shut her eyes for a moment, then reopened them. "I—I want to forget last night...and what happened."

"Well, I don't." His deep voice vibrated through her.

"None of this bothers you, does it? You're enjoying yourself."

Jeb's steady gaze met hers. "You're fun to watch when you sleep—when you're naked and soft and sweet with your legs all tangled up in mine."

"Will you shut up?"

A faint smile touched his lips.

"No."

"You've probably slept with so many women that one more or less is nothing to get excited about, but I'll have you know sex isn't just another casual sport for *me*."

"I could tell. You seemed to throw yourself into it

with total commitment. You were a most enthusiastic...er...athlete, and I found the game much more enjoyable than usual. You should take it up full-time.''

She ground her teeth. "I don't sleep around."

"Good. I wouldn't want any woman of mine to do that. What I was trying to say," he whispered huskily, "is that you should take it up full-time, but only with me."

"Never!"

He laughed good-naturedly. "While you were asleep I went to the hospital."

"You what?"

"You heard me. Kirk's conscious. He's hurting, but that hasn't changed his disposition. He's either complaining all the time or flirting with the nurses."

"He nearly died last night," Megan said.

"Well, he's very much alive this morning."

"You're exaggerating."

He smiled at her. "Only a little."

Megan felt weak with relief. She had forced herself to believe that her brother would live, but now that the danger was past, she realized how terrified she had been. Her whole body began to shake.

"Megan, about last night..."

She shrank beneath the sheets. "I don't feel like talking about it."

"Megan, just tell me this," Jeb demanded softly. "Do you hate me right now?"

Her eyes flew guiltily to his. There was a baffling gentleness about him this morning. When she thought of how he'd risked his own life to help her save Kirk, she knew her feelings for him would never again be as simple as the hatred she'd felt in the past.

"N-no," she admitted shakily.

Hard black eyes studied the torment etched on her pale face. He gripped her bare arms and pulled her closer against him.

"That's a start, at least," he muttered. The sheet fell away, and when she tried to retrieve it, his grip on her tightened.

She could feel his heart beginning to pound.

"Jeb," she murmured huskily, more seductively than she knew.

"Damn it. Stop being so stubborn and kiss me good morning," he said hoarsely. His gaze strayed to her lips as her tongue nervously moistened them.

She edged closer until her mouth hovered inches from his. She felt his body tense expectantly.

Then suddenly she realized what she was doing. More than anything she wanted to taste the salty sweetness of his skin, to know the hot, wet fever of his mouth devouring hers again.

She placed her fingers on his chest and shoved him away. Megan heard the harsh intake of his breath. He wanted her as much as she wanted him.

The sooner she ended this new turn their relationship had taken, the better.

She rolled away from him, wrapping the sheet around her naked body.

Swiftly he grabbed a corner of it. "If you try to get up, this is coming off."

"Jeb, let go, or at least turn your back so I can get dressed."

His eyes were brilliant. Brown fingers twisted the white tail of sheet. "You've got to be kidding, honey," he whispered. "After last night…"

"Last night changed nothing."

"Oh, but you're so wrong." His eyes, dark and unreadable, held hers. "So very wrong. It's changed everything."

He began unwinding the sheet from her lush, honey-gold body. She gave a shriek and tried to jump, but he grabbed her wrist and pulled her back. The sheet fell away.

His hands pressed her slim shoulders back, deep into the mattress. She struggled, kicking, fighting, twisting until she was out of breath. Then he fell on top of her, his own body hard and heavy, his breath coming fast. She felt his hands slide to her breasts and cup them.

His mouth covered hers, tasting her and then devouring her with a greedy passion. Megan opened her mouth.

"Megan. Megan."

Her name was a hot torrid whisper against the pounding pulse beat of her throat.

She was aching for him.

She couldn't let him do this. The arousal she felt was more than passion, more than simple desire. Every time he touched her the emotion seemed to feed on itself and grow. If she gave herself to him again, it would not stop her from wanting him but would tempt her all the more.

More than anything else now, Megan wanted love. It seemed that her whole life she had thirsted for it but had denied her need. She had lost her mother, her father and Kirk, in a way, to his stoic, macho silence. There hadn't been anyone for her to turn to, not for years.

Until last night.

In Jeb's arms.

The realization tore her into a million tiny pieces.

Only a foolish woman would think that sex would bind a man like Jeb Jackson to her. He would enjoy himself until he tired of the sport. Then he would marry another woman, one who could hold her own at elegant parties and who had the money he needed.

Megan lay stiffly on the bed, feeling too terribly insecure to surrender to her need for Jeb's tenderness.

He stroked her tumbled hair soothingly, and she cringed beneath the gentle caress of his fingers. She felt warier of him than she'd ever felt before—even when she'd hated him. To fall in love with a man who could never love her back would be a soul-destroying hell. It would be worse even than her father's leaving her. She mustn't allow this crazy attraction to go any further.

Jeb couldn't love her, and the cruelest irony of all was that last night it had been her touch that had seduced him.

He was a man. Naturally he had welcomed her passion, but it would be ridiculous to expect him to care, ridiculous to trust in her own new and dangerous feelings.

He continued to hold her, saying nothing, his hands never ceasing their gentle caress. If only he were a different kind of man and she could believe in his tenderness. If only she could bury her face in the hollow of his neck and cling to him endlessly.

With a sob she twisted away from him, wrapped herself in the sheet and ran into the bathroom.

Megan sat huddled in a chair near the window of Kirk's hospital room, her bright head drooping disconsolately as she listened to the whisper of the soft soles of the nurse's shoes on the tile floor. The private-duty nurse bustled about, plumping pillows, removing Kirk's breakfast tray, setting out his comb and other toilet articles.

Megan cast a quick, sidelong glance at her grim-faced brother and then turned back to stare gloomily out the window into the white glare. Kirk was sulking and wouldn't even look at her. Brilliant south Texas sunshine streamed through palm fronds and lit the lush semitropical vegetation around the hospital. Moodily Megan studied the scarlet bottle brush and lemon yellow hibiscus blossoms stirring in the faint breeze.

Seven days she had spent in this hospital. It felt like seven years.

Her manicured nail ticked against the windowsill.

Seven days of being ordered about by Jeb. Seven days of having to behave courteously to him as he popped in and out of Kirk's room whenever he pleased.

It was all Jeb's fault that she felt bored and useless. It was his fault, too, that she and Kirk were hardly speaking to each other.

Claiming that he didn't want her exhausting herself, Jeb had gone against Megan's wishes and hired nurses to sit with Kirk round-the-clock when he had been moved out of intensive care yesterday. Kirk had been furious that Megan hadn't been more grateful to Jeb. And Megan had been equally furious.

Why couldn't Kirk see that it had been her idea to fly down to Mexico? Why couldn't he see that her pride forbade her from accepting Jeb's generosity?

If only she hadn't slept with Jeb, maybe she wouldn't feel so miserable now. He seemed to delight in seizing every opportunity to remind her of their night together.

His eyes were hot and quick to seek her out whenever he was there. Every time he came into the room, his clean, male scent alone brought her back to the night he'd taken her in that pitch-black, icy motel room beneath that blood-red satin spread. Every time she caught even a glimpse of his broad shoulders and huge, muscled body she remembered how it had felt to be held against his warm, hair-roughened chest, her stomach pressed into his flat, hard-muscled belly as he thrust deep inside her.

Wanting him and not wanting to was agony. The tension was back in Megan's relationship with Jeb, only it was worse than ever before, worse even than when she'd had a high-school crush on him.

Why couldn't she simply erase him from her mind—and her heart and soul?

Just remembering that night was enough to make her mouth go dry with desire. She wanted him out of her life. Why didn't he go back to the ranch and do whatever he normally did to keep himself busy? Even his thoughtful treatment toward both Kirk and herself seemed part of his new threatening proprietary interest in her.

Since Kirk worked for the Jackson Ranch, the ranch's medical insurance policy was picking up Kirk's hospital bills. Jeb had flown in a special team of doctors from Houston to evaluate Kirk's case. In addition, there were the private-duty nurses.

Kirk was grateful to Jeb and angry at his sister because she wasn't. Only yesterday Kirk had quarreled with her over Jeb, and now Kirk had retreated inside his usual, noncommunicative, grim shell.

Her brother had nearly died. She'd risked her life to save him, and he had the gall to be mad at her! Megan no longer knew which man made her angrier—her brother or Jeb.

The hospital door banged open, and Jeb charged into the room.

Megan frowned, trying to block out the heady male vision of ink-dark hair, bronzed muscle, and an easy, flashing white smile. Jeb was a rogue, flagrantly challenging her right to deny his new importance in her life.

"Morning," Jeb boomed to both of them in a voice too loud to be politely ignored.

Megan turned her head impolitely away from his direction and ignored the greeting, anyway.

"Hi," Kirk murmured warmly.

There was a pregnant pause as both men waited for some sound from Megan.

She pressed her lips tightly together, and the tension mounted.

Kirk directed a dark scowl toward his stubborn, red-haired sister, but Megan wouldn't look at either of them. Instead she concentrated on a pool of sunlight trapped in the green pleats of a palm frond. She caught a choked breath when her brother's cheerful, deep voice broke the awkward silence.

"When are you going to pull some strings and get me out of here, Jeb?"

Megan's head whipped around. "Jeb's not your doctor."

"No, but he damn sure is the boss," Kirk replied.

Megan lunged out of her chair. She felt Jeb's black eyes raking over her again with devastating thoroughness. Color crept into her cheeks. "If Jeb pulls any strings like that, he'll have to fight me every step of the way."

"Don't tempt me, Megan." Jeb's voice cracked like a bullwhip. "Fighting you has always been one of my favorite sports." His mouth curved insolently. His eyes lingered on her breasts. "Among others."

Her body burned from head to toe. She couldn't stay here and endure his presence! Then she became aware of Kirk watching her, his dark face tightly strained.

"I think I'll go to the coffee shop," she rasped, struggling for control.

"I'd rather you stayed," Jeb said quietly.

"I'd rather go, but I guess my feelings about things don't matter much."

"Stay, Megan," Kirk ordered, "and stop picking on Jeb."

"Me?" She expelled a stifled gasp. "Picking?" She stared at Kirk in slack-mouthed wonder, began to defend herself, but then stopped. Kirk looked too tired and drawn to fight.

"Jeb," Kirk apologized, "I don't know what's gotten into her. I would have thought she'd show you a little gratitude—since you saved my life."

"K-Kirk!" Megan bit back the hot, angry words that sprang to her lips.

"Don't worry, she has been grateful—in her own way," Jeb said, a wealth of meaning in his silken voice.

Megan's eyes flew to Jeb's face. He had turned in her direction so that only she could catch his knowing smile.

Megan swallowed and took an instinctive step backward.

"I'd still be down in that hellhole if you hadn't come after me," Kirk said. "I owe you one, Jeb, and I won't forget it."

"It wasn't his idea to come after you," Megan snapped. "You'd still be down there if I—"

"Jeb carried me out of that hut." Kirk's voice was edged with steel. "Jeb got shot and got his Mooney shot up, too."

"And I did nothing?"

"I didn't say that," Kirk replied more gently.

Megan remembered that wild, dark night, the flickering flares, the desolate whir of the Mooney's prop when she'd been left alone with the plane in the black jungle, the army that had shot at them. Mutely she shook her head, trying to erase the memories that brought back soul-gnawing fear. She went to her brother's bed and took his hand in hers.

"Kirk, please, I don't like remembering how close I came to losing you. Please, say you won't ever do anything like that again, no matter how much money you're offered."

"It's not just the money," Kirk said grimly.

"I know." Her fingers squeezed his. "But I can't bear the thought of something happening to you."

Kirk's lips tightened fractionally. "So you're trying to catch me in a weak moment and extract a promise." The words were quiet. His expression was unreadable.

Megan swallowed and nodded guiltily.

"Well, you damn sure picked the right moment." His knuckles slid against the inside of her palm. "I never look forward to going, but when someone's in trouble, and I think I can help…" Kirk's stubbled jaw clenched. "Megan, don't ask me to make a promise I can't keep." His brooding eyes met hers.

From behind them came Jeb's silky-smooth voice. "Speaking of someone in trouble—Dwight Creighton is out in the hall waiting to thank you, Kirk. I think I'll buy Megan a cup of coffee while the two of you visit."

Mutely Megan shook her head. "I don't want coffee."

Jeb's black eyes seemed to ice over. "I'm sure we can find some place that sells herbal tea or…"

"That's not what I meant."

Beneath his faintly mocking smile, Jeb's mouth hardened.

"Megan," Kirk asked gently in a tired voice, "please, for me, try to be nice to Jeb. Just this once."

"You MacKays never learn. You're always demanding the impossible of each other." Jeb laughed. "Don't worry, Kirk, I can handle Megan." Jeb's hot gaze fell on Megan's slim figure.

Megan felt the bold sweep of his eyes. From across the room she glared back at him. She had taken more of his leers and innuendo than any woman could. Not even for Kirk would she endure more. She got up and strode swiftly toward the door.

Cowboy boots clamored behind her. With ruthless ease Jeb's hands clamped around her shoulders and waist and yanked her against his body. "I'm glad you decided to accept my invitation," Jeb murmured dryly, holding her tightly.

"I—I didn't."

Pain cut off all speech as hard fingers tightened against soft flesh. She winced as he lifted her on to her toes and ushered her down the hall.

In the deserted waiting room, Jeb exploded. "Why did you check out of the motel and move in with that college girlfriend of yours?"

Defiant green eyes met his. "You were trying to force something on me that I don't want, Jeb."

He drew a ragged breath. "You're the most stubborn woman I've ever known."

She started to move away, but he pushed her back against the wall, holding her fiercely.

"Someone might come, Jeb."

"Do you think I give a damn?" he whispered. "You're trying to push me away, trying to pretend that what happened between us never happened."

"Because it was a mistake!"

"It happened!"

"Don't! Please!"

"And you loved it."

The awful, galling truth shamed her utterly.

His fingers ruffled through her hair. She could feel his breath, hot against her temple.

"I loved it too, Megan, and I can't forget it. Every time I look at you I remember the taste of your mouth, the woman-scent of your body, the silken fire of your skin, and I want you all over again."

"N-no. It was only sex. You don't own me."

"Damn!" He lifted a hand and trailed his fingertips down the side of her neck and watched her shiver. "Would it be so bad—belonging to me?" he said thickly. His hand slid lower, against her throat, to the swelling curve of her breast.

Her pulse was pounding like a drum. She felt hot and breathless. She jerked away from his touch.

"It would be a living hell," she whispered.

He pulled her to him. "You're driving me crazy. You know that, don't you?"

The passion that shone in his eyes shook Megan to the core. She closed her eyes, attempting to shut him out, but she couldn't block out the heat of him. She opened them again at once, only to discover that he had come even nearer.

"You're driving me crazy, too."

"So why doesn't one of us stop?" he demanded softly.

Jeb was so close. His clean scent enveloped her, and the memory of the night she had slept with him drove her wild. It would be all too easy to melt against him.

She tried to back away, but there was nowhere to go. "Look, I'm not going to become your latest ranch plaything, a toy you can toss aside when you're no longer amused."

The hard line of his mouth tightened. "You make me sound like a spoiled child."

"In a way, you are. You're used to pushing everyone around. You pushed me around for years."

"You needed more discipline than you ever got."

"You grew up rich."

"But not spoiled. Wayne Jackson never spoiled any living creature on Jackson Ranch. I worked damn hard. I still do."

"You've had everything you ever wanted."

His eyes fixed on her hungrily. His voice was a hoarse whisper. "Not everything."

"I mean...till now."

"Be fair, Megan. You know I've worked as hard as the lowest vaquero."

"But you're the boss. Who has ever said no to you?"

"You did."

"You always got your way in the end."

"Because I was right and you were just plain stubborn."

"That's your opinion. The point is, now you've decided you want me. Well, I've wanted things, too. Only there were a lot of things I couldn't have. Maybe you've finally hit on something you can't have. A long time ago you won my ranch and me in a game of five-card stud. You took my ranch. The other night you finally took me."

"Took you?" he growled, taking her hand and pulling her close, holding on to it fiercely when she fought to wrench it free. "I'm damned if I'll take the blame for that. You seduced me."

"It's obvious you intend to hold that over my head forever. Maybe I was grateful that night because you saved Kirk," she admitted stubbornly. "I don't know. But now I don't owe you anything. You'll never take anything else from me again. All I ask is that you don't brag to everybody on the ranch about how easy I was!"

"Brag!" he snarled. "You little fool, I've given you more than I've ever taken."

"You're the fool, Jeb, to waste your time on me. You're going to marry Janelle. She's richer than I am, and she'll fit in with all your classy friends. It's no secret you need money to run the ranch. All I ever want to do for you is fly your airplanes."

Against the extreme pallor of his face, his eyes were deep and dark and insolent. "Is that what you think I want?"

"You'll have the perfect, obedient wife, a transfusion of money for the ranch and an excellent pilot. Besides, Janelle wants you. I don't."

"Don't you?" Without thinking, he yanked her roughly into his arms and kissed her, his hard mouth forcing hers to open to him. "Was one night really enough for you? You were wild in my arms. I can't forget how you begged me to—"

"No!" The memory of every word, every touch, every sighing moan haunted Megan.

"You were made for a man's kisses, a man's loving."

"Not yours!" She broke away. "You had me once, but playtime's over."

"Playtime!" A muscle twitched furiously in Jeb's cheek. "I risked my life for you, helped you get Kirk out of Mexico, got my new Mooney shot up and broke dozens of international laws. Doesn't that mean anything to you?"

"N-no. I don't want you. Maybe I had a crush on you when I was a kid, but I don't anymore."

A fierce, unnameable emotion was in her eyes and in her heart.

He studied her ashen face for a long, silent moment.

"All right. Have it your own way. You can fly my airplanes. That's all I'll ever ask of you."

Megan glared back at him with a heady mixture of disbelief and triumph. She'd never thought victory would come so easily.

He read her mind. The corners of his mouth quirked sardonically. "Maybe I'll even take your advice and marry Janelle."

His casual remark was like a knife thrust in the softest tissue of her heart.

"The sooner the better," Megan whispered.

Steady black eyes seared her soul. "Then you wouldn't mind flying Janelle from California to Texas for my birthday party in a few weeks?"

"No," Megan said, too quickly. She tossed her head in an abrupt motion. "Why should I?"

"Just asking," came his cool reply.

He turned and stalked away indifferently.

Her heart wanted to call him back, but her mind reined in the impulse.

He pulled open the waiting-room door and a cold draft swept inside.

Then he was gone, and she was left staring mutely at the closed door.

Seven

The Porsche roared across desolate ranch land beneath a star-beaded, ink-black canopy of sky. It wasn't late, but it looked like it was because in southern Texas, as in the tropics, there was no lingering twilight. Blazing suns melted into nights as black and hot as pitch.

Megan's hair whipped about her face in the warm humid wind that smelled of mesquite and huisache, cattle and dry earth. She felt Byrom's fingers move beneath her flying hair to caress the sensitive skin at the nape of her neck.

Once she would have edged closer to him when he caressed her like that, but tonight she twisted away with a shudder. He stiffened at her rejection, pulled his hand away and replaced it on the steering wheel. The pointed toe of his boot jammed the accelerator to the floorboard, and the car leapt forward, tearing crazily down the black ribbon of road.

She knew she had hurt him, but she couldn't help it. All evening she had felt strange and jittery every time he'd even lightly touched her.

He expected her to move closer, to take his hand, to smile at him invitingly, to apologize for the way she was behaving. Instead she remained rigidly where she was, staring into the silent darkness, wishing everything could be as it was before that night with Jeb. But she knew nothing would ever be the same again.

"I understand you're pretty upset about Kirk," Byrom said quietly, after a long time.

Gratefully she seized on the excuse he had provided. "Yes."

Byrom kept talking along the same vein, his soothing words scarcely audible above the powerful roar of the car. After a while she stopped trying to listen. Oh, why did she keep thinking longingly of a dark-faced man, as male as one of his great champion bulls, as stubborn as any mule; a man whose velvet drawl fell as softly on her ears as a musical caress?

It had been a month now since she'd slept with Jeb.

And two days since he'd sent her to California to pick up Janelle and bring her to Texas for his upcoming birthday. Though Megan hadn't actually seen him with the softly golden and demure Janelle, she had felt tortured by the knowledge that they were together.

Tonight Megan had gone out with Byrom to forget Jeb.

But all she had done was think about him incessantly.

True to his word, Jeb had avoided her and turned to Janelle. Instead of relieved, Megan felt tormented.

Byrom cut the engine in front of the MacKay cottage, got out of the car and walked Megan to the door. They stood together, spotlighted in the golden cone of the porch light. The muted sounds of the television came from inside. Out of the corner of her eye she saw a movement as a dark, furled curtain fell back in place at the window.

Byrom pulled her into his arms, and his skillful mouth played over hers.

A sudden burst of male laughter from inside the house robbed her of the ability to concentrate on Byrom's kiss. His mouth felt cold, alien on hers. Gently she pushed him away.

"Sounds like your brother has company," Byrom said mildly.

From inside she heard her name huskily spoken, and the sound electrified her.

"Megan and I don't always fight," came that low melodious tone. "There have been times…"

She would have known that purring, sardonic drawl anywhere. Her heart began to pound like a frightened rabbit's, even as her mind desperately tried to deny Jeb's presence. Her golden skin paled, and her eyes glowed with an almost feverish brightness.

How dared Jeb speak of her in such a way—to her own brother—and so loud she and her date could hear him outside on the porch?

A tom-tom was beating in her breast.

She had told Jeb she wanted him to stay away. And yet...

"Good night, Byrom," Megan said, stiffening so she wouldn't tremble.

"Good night?" Byrom's quizzical blond brows shot upward. Usually she invited him inside.

She lowered her eyes with a demureness she was far from feeling. "Good night," she said with grim finality. "My boss, Jeb Jackson, is inside. I'd better find out what he wants."

"Saturday night then?"

"Okay." She nodded, frantic for him to leave. "Saturday night."

Then he was gone.

Megan threw the door open and slammed it behind her violently.

Two Indian-dark men swiveled in their chairs.

She tipped her head back and gazed defiantly into Jeb's handsome face. "What do you want?"

"Careful," Jeb purred in a low, lazy voice that

made her heart pound even faster. "That's my house you're treating so roughly."

"We'll move if that's what you want," Megan snapped. She set her crimson scarf and her purse on a table and tried to tidy her hair with shaking hands.

"Can't you be nice to Jeb this once?" Kirk asked.

Jeb's eyes devoured her slowly, boldly evaluating every curve of her visible assets—and too many were visible in the strapless scarlet evening dress that fit her body like a glove.

Jeb's sunburned face broke into an insolent grin that stretched from his mouth to his eyes. He watched the rapid rise and fall of her breasts pushing against the shimmering red cloth. For the first time she wished she'd worn something less dramatic, less revealing.

"You look good in red," he murmured.

Was that a compliment or an insult? She didn't know how to react, so she merely acknowledged him with a cold look that only made his white grin broaden and his eyes gleam.

Slowly his long, silent gaze kindled a new fire in her. Was one look all it took for Jeb Jackson to undress a woman?

"Been dancing instead of taking care of your brother, I see," Jeb taunted silkily.

An electric hostility charged the air between them.

"Kirk insisted," she bristled hotly. "Tell him, Kirk."

"Did I? I don't remember. I'm staying out of this one, little sister," her brother said dryly.

"You know you did!"

"There's no need to shout at Kirk, Megan." Jeb's black eyes flashed with amusement. "A simple yes or no will do. Besides, no need to worry. I kept Kirk company…while you were out. Had there been an emergency—"

She glared into Jeb's jeering, dark face. "You of all people have no right to judge me."

Megan marched toward the kitchen, determined to escape him, but Jeb was right behind her.

"I'm not judging," he whispered. "I'm just observing. And while I am, your lipstick's smeared and your hair is a mess."

She whirled. "So? Who cares?"

His eyes darkened to midnight black.

Megan would have given anything to be able to pretend he wasn't there, but he moved closer, filling the kitchen with his virile presence. She was too disturbingly conscious of him.

"I do," he whispered.

"What about Janelle?"

The creases around his mouth hardened. "Forget Janelle," he ground out harshly.

"You have no right. You promised—"

He stared at Megan for a long moment. Her hair fell about her shoulders in wild red ribbons of flame.

Her lips were soft and mussed from another man's kiss.

A muscle twitched in his jaw. "That doesn't seem to matter anymore," Jeb muttered raggedly.

She glanced down, away from the hot darkness of his compelling gaze. For the first time Megan noticed that Jeb was holding the carved wooden figure of herself and him that her father had carved. Megan's eyes lifted again, questioningly, to Jeb's.

She no longer understood herself. She had wanted him out of her life. For two weeks he had completely ignored her, and she had been miserable. Now, in the kitchen, alone with him, she felt nervously excited, curiously exhilarated.

Her gaze fell to the carving again. The wooden figure in his brown hand evoked bittersweet memories she would have preferred to forget. Glen had whittled the piece shortly before he had lost the ranch. Megan had adored Jeb then. She'd been sixteen, a child, and yet not a child at all. The sweetness that had passed between them was something she wanted to erase from her mind, but every time she looked at the carved figures, she remembered that afternoon with a deep and poignant nostalgia.

She snatched the carving from him, and as she did, their fingers touched. A delicious shiver danced over her skin. She jerked her hand from his, but not before liquid fire had flashed from his caress.

His gaze ran over her face, black and glinting. Then

Jeb reached up and brushed her lips with a fingertip. "I've fancied that piece for years, Megan."

The subtle inflection of eroticism in his low tone deepened the color in her face and made a golden fire race in her veins. Something elemental seemed to hover in the air, charging it with tension.

"It's a particular favorite of mine," he said. "It brings back memories. I never realized before how much I cherished them."

He made a deep study of her mouth and the rounded swell of her breasts. His smoldering look made her blood pulse with excitement.

"You're the last person on earth I'd believe to have a sentimental nature."

"So you remember that day, too?" His hand settled on her bare shoulder possessively.

"No!" she whispered tightly, even as she was drawn by a magnetic force that somehow emanated from him. "Let me go."

He smoothed her wild hair with his fingers. When he had finished, he nestled her head against the curve of his throat. "We walked down to the beach. The sun was like fire in your hair. You picked up so many shells we didn't have enough hands to carry them back. I remember you weaving wildflowers into your hair."

She felt his lips against her temple, his warm breath falling rhythmically against her hair, and she was no longer struggling. She wanted him to go on holding her, to go on talking forever.

His hand curved along her slender throat and he turned her face toward his. "Then," he continued huskily, "comes my favorite part…"

"Stop!"

Jeb's eyes touched hers, and she knew he was remembering that young, eager kiss, her first. She had loved him so desperately, so childishly. She hadn't known then how unscrupulous he was. He'd accepted her kiss, then gently set her aside.

"So you do remember?" he whispered teasingly.

"No…"

"Liar. I was a fool not to take what you freely offered. I was trying to be noble. I'd take it now." There was leashed passion in his husky tone. "Gladly."

His lips followed the dark line of a winged brow, and she seemed to stop breathing at the velvet warmth of his mouth tracing along her skin.

"Megan…" His voice was low, urgent.

She felt the pressure of his hand near the small of her back as he arched her toward him. His mouth closed over her parted lips, and she could taste the vague, curiously pleasant flavor of his cigarettes.

The hard muscles of his chest flattened her breasts. Through the thin red dress she could feel the violent thudding of his heart.

Her fingers curved around his neck, into the silken

black thickness of his hair. Jeb lifted his head a fraction of an inch, and their hot breath mingled when he spoke. "Open your mouth, Megan. I want to taste you."

His hard lips claimed hers again. In the hot, wet fullness of the kiss, wildfire raced through her arteries. Her bones seemed to melt, and she clung to him limply. An instinct that was fierce and wild and pure had taken her over.

When Jeb dragged his mouth from hers a long time later, his taut voice trembled hoarsely against the slender column of her throat. She felt the blistering heat of his skin touching hers.

"Glen watched us come back laughing and running. Then he sat down on the porch and was quiet for a spell while he whittled that out of a block of wood. I'd give anything to have it, Megan. I'd pay anything…"

He was holding her, not kissing her, and she struggled against the primitive desire exploding within her.

"It's not for sale."

There was a faint grimness about his sun-bronzed features. "Megan…"

Jeb was about to kiss her again, and she knew if he did, she'd never be able to fight her way out of the whirlpool of passion he could so easily evoke.

Stiffening with fear, Megan wrenched herself free and ran back to the living room. Kirk looked up from a magazine as she clumsily thrust the wooden figure back on its shelf, knocking over two others.

His sister's eyes were blazing. Her normally pale face was livid with emotion.

"You giving Jeb a hard time again?" Kirk demanded.

Jeb stalked into the room after her.

"Jeb, sorry if Megan's got it in for you. She really can be fun when she's not as mad as ten hornets."

Jeb grinned. His gaze slid to her trembling mouth. "She certainly can be."

Megan bit her lips and refused to look at either of them.

"The figure's yours, Jeb," Kirk said generously, "if you want it. All it does here is gather dust."

"It's not yours to give, Kirk," Megan said.

Kirk threw his magazine on the table with grim resolve. "Wouldn't you say it's little enough to pay for your brother's life?"

"I never realized the piece was a favorite of yours, too, Megan," Jeb said softly, mockingly.

"It isn't one of my favorites!" she lied.

"Then why are you so determined to hold on to it?" Jeb's voice was velvet smooth; his eyes too knowing.

"Because Glen gave it to me! He gave me little enough. You took everything else that had any real value."

Kirk stared at her, appalled. He started to say something, but she cut him off before he could begin to lecture her. "And you just sat back and let Jeb take it, Kirk MacKay. You're always rushing off to fight for strangers. Why didn't you fight for what was ours?"

"The ranch was Glen's," Kirk said, his low voice hard-edged. "Not mine. Or yours, Megan. If he wanted to gamble away what was left of it in a poker game, I figured it was his to gamble. Gambling always gave him more pleasure than those scrap acres ever did. Besides, after Mother left, I never cared much for the place. I don't think Glen did, either. Maybe if he'd have moved to town and taken a job, Mother would have stayed."

"I'll never understand why you went to work for Jeb after he took—"

"Maybe 'cause I was tired of fighting. Trouble with you is you've never gotten the fighting out of your system. Jeb's sheltered and protected you all your life. He's spoiled you, Megan."

"Jeb...spoiled... Come on, Kirk!"

"No, you listen for once. When I went away, I asked him to take care of you, and he did."

"You what?"

"I knew I couldn't trust Glen to do it."

"Don't say those things about Daddy!"

"It's the truth. You always had a knack for getting into trouble. Glen never was much good at stopping you. The reason you were usually mad at Jeb was because he was keeping you out of it.''

She opened her mouth and closed it again.

''And when I came home, even though he couldn't afford to, Jeb gave me a job. And more important, he gave me some time and space to forget. Jeb's been the closest thing to a friend you or I have ever had. I keep hoping that one day you'll have the sense to see it.''

''Sometimes I don't have any use for either of you!'' Her eyes glittered briefly from Kirk to Jeb. Then she stormed to her bedroom and slammed the door.

''She sure is hell on doors,'' Jeb said innocently.

''Be glad it's only doors,'' Kirk replied with big-brotherly indifference. ''She's sure been unusually cranky for the past two weeks, too. You'd think she'd be glad I wasn't shot to bits. I guess it shook her up when you brought me back to the plane half dead and those guys started shooting. I've seen soldiers crack up under less pressure than that. Jeb, you can have that statue. I'll straighten things out with Megan after you're gone.''

Jeb expelled a harsh breath. ''No, I won't take anything from Megan that she doesn't give me willingly. But it's getting late, and you're looking tired. By the way, don't forget that the main reason I stopped by was because I wanted to remind Megan and you to be sure and come to my birthday party Saturday.''

"We wouldn't miss it for the world."

From the other side of the door there was the sound of something shattering against a hard floor.

Megan flung open the bedroom door. Her hair still tumbled in wild disarray. She'd changed into Kirk's overlarge green shirt again. "I'd miss it, gladly!"

"I thought you'd gone to bed," Jeb said dryly, coming up to her and smiling with perverse pleasure as he let his hot insolent gaze roam over the length of her. "I should've known you'd have your ear pressed to the door till I left."

A dull red flush crept over her fair skin. "I have a date Saturday night," she said heatedly.

The line of Jeb's mouth thinned harshly. "Bring him along."

"But..."

"I insist." Contempt was audible in his demand.

More than anything she wanted to refuse.

"I did save your brother," Jeb added, "or doesn't that mean anything?"

Her skin went white. Her eyes were icy-green glitter. Kirk was watching her closely.

How dare Jeb accuse her of not caring for Kirk! A dozen hot insults leapt to her tongue.

"Megan!" Kirk warned. "Say you'll go...for me."

Megan was about to protest, but as she glanced toward her brother, she saw that despite his massive build, he looked gray with fatigue. He wanted her to go and there was no way she could refuse.

Megan nodded slowly in defeat.

Jeb watched her, his black eyes narrowing thoughtfully.

"I guess that settles that," Jeb declared, picking up his Stetson and planting it on his gleaming black head. Under his breath as he passed her, he growled, "I win as usual."

Eight

At the top of the stairs Megan hesitated, feeling ridiculously awkward and out of her depth as she waited for Byrom to park the car. In one hand she clutched a small, brightly wrapped birthday present. The elegant party had already started, and she was thankful that Wayne and Mercedes Jackson had finished receiving guests and that their places beneath the glittering chandelier in the foyer stood empty.

Byrom rushed up the stairs and pressed Megan's clammy hand in his. "Thought I'd never find a parking place."

Megan tried to smile at him and felt only a painful pulling at the corners of her mouth.

A chattering group of young women in silks, chiffons and flashing jewels flew past them and disappeared into the house. Kirk was already inside.

Brilliant floodlights lit the house so that the red-roofed Spanish mansion stood out like a radiant ruby set with diamonds against the velvet blackness of the night. A constant stream of helicopters and limousines had ferried wealthy guests from the airport.

For a week Megan had dreaded this night. For a week everyone else on the ranch had hummed with excitement over the party. The house was filled with caterers and bartenders and extra help hired to serve. White party tents had been erected beside the pool.

Mariachis were outside strumming their guitars, and the hauntingly melodious Mexican music filled Megan with an aching nostalgia for other evenings, simpler evenings when she had danced until dawn with the cowboys in their sharply pressed, razor-edged khakis and laughed and talked with the dark-skinned women and children.

It was the Jackson Ranch custom to give two parties simultaneously in celebration of all grand occasions. Thus, whenever there was a party at the Big House, there was one given outside for the ranch hands, too. Usually it was the ranch-hand party that Megan attended, instead of the more formal affair at the Big House. Tonight, more than ever before, she would have preferred the outdoor party.

As she stepped inside the door, Megan heard the

strains of the orchestra from the ballroom, and her heart tightened with a feeling of queer, almost painful expectancy as she thought of seeing Jeb again. She had bought a new dress, a bright emerald-green gown with long, swirling skirts that seemed to float at her every turn. Nestled against the flyaway tendrils of her flame-red hair was a yellow blossom that Kirk had picked and given to her from the vine of climbing roses that grew beneath her bedroom window.

She remembered his hushed words, velvet soft in the darkness. "Be happy tonight, Megan. For me."

She had nodded, unable to speak.

"And try to be nice to Jeb. He cares more about you than you know."

She had turned away.

Megan felt uneasy surrounded by the opulence of Jeb's house and the glamour and sophistication of his guests. There was nothing like one of Mercedes's elegant parties to show Megan the gulf that separated the Jacksons from their employees.

Elegant gifts with golden labels from fancy stores completely covered the vast, polished library table in the foyer beneath the dazzling chandelier. Quickly, before anyone could see her humble, squashed package, she darted forward and tucked it beneath the rest of the presents.

At the last minute she had snatched the wooden figure that Jeb had always wanted from the shelf, wrapping it clumsily while Byrom had tapped his foot impatiently, fuming while he waited in the living room.

No matter how she felt about Jeb, it was his birthday. He had risked his life to save Kirk, and she had wanted him to have something special from her. Now, as she studied the fashionable pile of professionally wrapped gifts with the soft lights glinting off their green, red and yellow satin bows, she wished she'd left her humble present at home. Her gift seemed as out of place in the elegant mound as did she with her simple gown and rose in her hair among Jeb's bejeweled guests.

A girl called to Byrom, and he left Megan for a moment. The broad, gleaming doors between the library, the drawing room and ballroom stood open wide so that guests could spill easily from one room to the next, and already the old-fashioned rooms with their quarter-sawn oak-paneled walls and their lovely white Gothic ceilings were jammed with people. Waiters served bourbon and Scotch, old-fashioneds and martinis. Straight bourbon was the favorite among the Texan men.

In the library several politicians were speaking a little too loudly to groups that had clustered around them. The conversation centered on border problems, water shortages, bank foreclosures and the troubles in the oil business. But Megan took no notice. She was looking for Jeb.

On a whirl of music the dancers at the edge of the

ballroom spun and parted. She saw him. Her mouth suddenly felt dry.

Hundreds of attractive faces, glittering gowns and sparkling jewels blurred. Across the ballroom floor, she saw only one darkly handsome, virile male.

He was so tall, so swarthy, so magnificently built he stood apart even though he wore a black tux and black tie like most of the other men. Megan could feel the pull of his animal magnetism welling up inside her. Her breath caught painfully in her throat, and she couldn't swallow.

He was dancing with Janelle. Megan's breath again came quickly, and her heart began to pound high in her throat.

Janelle's golden head was tilted so that her shining curls, wound with lustrous pearls, cascaded down her back. Through her long lashes she gazed into his black eyes. Her exquisite face was rapt. She was all in red. Her gown, with its low neck and straight-cut skirt that clung to her slim figure, was stylish and boldly dramatic. A strand of pearls lay against the soft curves of her bosom. Jeb's black head was bent attentively over her fair one, and she laughed gaily at something he murmured into her ear, tossing her head so that a single, perfectly formed silver coil dangled over her shoulder. He was holding her very close, as if he never wanted to let her go.

Megan's head began to throb dully as the blood rushed to it, her stomach feeling as if a knife had been plunged into it. Her feet and hands had gone numb, and she was shivering with cold. But she could not drag her eyes away from them.

Megan was not the only one watching. They were such an arresting couple that many an eyebrow arched speculatively in their wake. Tomorrow they would be a delicious item of gossip.

Megan imagined the whispered, titillating conversations.

Isn't she a stunning creature.

No more than he.

He'll never do better.

And he has that ambition to marry well.

Megan turned her face to the wall, but she could not block out the image of Janelle, beautiful and polished and sophisticated in her designer gown and pearls. A fitting queen for a man who considered himself a king. By comparison Megan felt shabbily flamboyant, wearing no other jewel than the yellow rose in her hair.

Clumsily she removed the blossom and cast it toward a nearby table, not caring when she tangled her hair and the rose fell instead to the floor where it would no doubt be crushed carelessly under some guest's booted heel. She glanced up, and Jeb's eyes met hers.

Megan wanted to turn away, to stop watching the handsome man in black tails whirl the golden woman lightly in his arms, but she was fascinated. She felt a quick, jealous heat rise and ebb in her cheeks, leaving her even colder than before. Her face was the color of starched linen, her eyes dull green emeralds without sparkle, her emotions plain for him to read.

"Megan, don't stand there like a wallflower where everyone can see you eating your heart out," rasped Nick Browning from behind her. "It's high time you figured out that you're in love with my big brother."

She whirled. "I'm not in—" When she tried to smile lightly into that familiar tanned face beneath the butter-gold hair, her mouth merely quivered and the denial would not come.

Nick's grin was bold enough for both of them. He was flashily dressed in a white tux with a peacock-blue shirt that intensified the color of his vivid, sparkling eyes. His hair was streaked silver from the many days he spent racing and sailing all over the world. He had just flown in from a week-long series of races off Bermuda.

He swept her into his arms in a bear hug and let her go. Megan had grown up loving Nick as a brother. He'd always taken time to be kind to her when he came to the ranch every summer to visit his father Wayne Jackson and his half brothers, Jeb and Tad.

She looked at him inquiringly. "I didn't realize you were coming."

"I received a royal summons from the king himself," Nick teased. "I had no choice but to obey."

"I never realized before you had such an obedient nature."

He laughed. Heads turned. She was aware of Jeb and Janelle dancing nearer to them. Of Jeb's eyes seeking hers.

"You know me too well," Nick said.

"Where's Amy?"

Nick was Jeb's younger illegitimate brother. He'd been born during a lengthy separation between Mercedes and Wayne in the early years of their turbulent marriage. Jeb and Nick had resented each other from the first. They had been like two young bucks fighting over the same scrap of territory.

Nick laughed easily again. "Amy's got her eye glued to Triple."

Triple was the liveliest child Megan had ever encountered. On his last visit to the ranch, Triple had sneaked into Megan's Piper and taxied down the runway because he'd read how to fly in a comic book and wanted to try it. Fortunately he'd run out of runway before he'd managed to take off. This afternoon he'd gotten clunked in the head by a stray hoof while trying to shoe his pony.

"More than one eye, I hope! Triple's a full-time job."

Nick grinned. "You don't know the half of it. Right now he's at the hors d'oeuvres table gobbling up all those tiny meatballs. Amy's afraid if she leaves him for a second he'll get into trouble. He's got a bigger appetite for mischief than he does for meat-balls.''

"I haven't forgotten the day he stowed away on Jeb's jet and came to Texas."

A glow of happiness deepened the color of Nick's eyes. "Well, at least that crisis brought Amy and me back together."

"You three are doing okay then?"

"If you call expecting a baby okay." Nick beamed with paternal pride.

"After producing Triple, I'd say that's living dangerously."

Nick laughed indulgently. "I thought you were the girl who didn't know any other way to live."

"I'm not the wild hellion you used to know."

"Really?" Nick frowned in mock disappointment.

"I'm not!"

"Dance with me, Megan."

"I..."

He took her hand in his. "It will make Jeb jealous."

"But I don't want—"

His bold blue eyes saw through to her heart. "Why not, when that same emotion is eating you alive?"

"Nick—"

Nick's eyes twinkled. "Besides, I'd kind of like to stir big brother up a bit—for old times' sake. I've been too easy on him lately."

"But your wife—"

"My wife has no doubts that I adore her."

Megan was in Nick's hard arms. He danced expertly, as he did everything else. Megan caught more than a few curious looks cast in their direction, but she didn't care.

She said breathlessly, "You don't really have to dance with me, you know. I—"

"Don't be an idiot!" He laughed.

Megan was busy trying to find Jeb in the crowd, to see him without actually catching his eye. When she found him at last, he was kneeling down beside the table where she'd thrown her rose, retrieving it reverently, pinning it to his lapel. As he stood his eyes met hers. Her throat constricted as she saw the tensing of his muscles as he looked at her.

A split second later Nick whirled her around, and their eyes were torn apart. Jeb was lost in the throng.

Nick and Megan were dancing at the periphery of the crowd, near the great doors leading to the solarium, and before Megan quite knew what was happening, he had pushed the doors open and pulled her through them. They slipped out easily and unnoticeably into the darkened room, moonlight streaming through its skylights. The music followed them softly, muted, as was the rumble of laughter and conversation of the guests.

The solarium smelled of roses and orchids and gardenias. Megan's skirts brushed the petals of a potted azalea bush. They danced down the length of the room where soaring columns cast long shadows, and the music seemed a long way off.

Nick stopped in the darkest corner.

"If this doesn't do it, nothing will," Nick said under his breath.

Megan was too breathless from dancing to catch his meaning.

The moonlight shone in Nick's butter-gold hair. "So how did it happen—your discovery that you love Jeb?" Nick demanded. "Did he seduce you?"

From the shadows behind them came a stern, all-too-familiar voice. "It was the other way around."

"Speak of the devil…" Nick's goading voice trailed away on a note of satisfied triumph. "Happy birthday!"

Jeb's face looked hard and remote, his body rigid. "Do you mind if I join you, or would three be a crowd?"

"Megan and I were just catching up on old times," Nick replied softly, obtusely.

"So that's what you call it." Jeb edged closer, looming out of the shadows. He smiled at her, a terrible, aristocratic, condescending smile. Megan could hear the anger, barely leashed, in his voice.

His sinewy hand reached through the moonlight and closed around her forearm. "Your Dr. Ferguson was looking for you a while ago."

She arched her eyebrows coolly. "Oh?"

"He was called away on a medical emergency. He

said he might not be able to get back. He couldn't find you to tell you himself.''

''Is that why you followed us out here?''

''That was one reason.'' Behind Jeb's veiled look Megan felt the dark intensity of his gaze. He turned to regard his brother with equal intensity.

Nick smiled at him lazily. ''I think you're right. Three is a crowd.''

Nick melted into the darkness. The last thing to disappear was his warm, teasing grin.

''And…your other reasons…for following us?'' Megan murmured shakily.

For a pregnant moment he didn't speak. Megan could not stop looking at him. She could see the faint shadow that darkened his jaw. His recent injury where the bullet had grazed his temple had left no mark. But she could see the faint edges of a tiny scar beside his left brow, and her face whitened with guilt. During roundup last spring, he had ordered her about, and she had gotten so mad she had buzzed him with her plane when he was riding Caesar. Caesar had gone wild and thrown him. She had expected Jeb to fire her on the spot, but he had lain in the back of his pickup, his dark face grim and bloodied and accepted her stammering apology as if the incident were nothing. Then he'd ordered Mario to drive him to the hospital. He had needed the stitches of a plastic surgeon.

The scent of the yellow rose in his lapel came to

her nostrils. It was sweet and delicate. Her rose. His wearing it seemed an intimate thing.

"I had to be alone with you," he whispered. Something flared in his eyes, then vanished. He was in the grip of some powerful emotion. The muscles along his jaw whitened from his effort to control it.

For an instant she was moved by his words, by the passion in his low tone. Then she remembered his dancing with Janelle. He made love to whatever woman he was with. But given the choice, he would marry money.

"But I don't want to be alone with you," she managed tightly, taking several faltering steps back.

"You could at least wish me a happy birthday," he said. He followed her as she darted for the doors, gripping her by the arm and spinning her around. His arms circled her, crushing her to his length. Soft emerald skirts floated in the air. Her hair was like a wing of flame.

His touch felt like fire, like ice, a volt of sensation sizzling through her, numbing her will to fight.

"Happy birth—"

Megan looked past him. A woman in red opened the door and stood framed in a bright rectangle of golden light, calling softly to Jeb.

As she recognized Janelle, Megan's tongue seemed to stick to the roof of her mouth. She stared at Jeb in mute anguish.

He had had only to touch her to prove she was his. But he could never be hers. It wasn't fair!

Suddenly, surprising them both, she spoke in a low strangled voice. "Let Janelle wish you happy birthday." Megan jerked free of his grasp, and, gathering her skirts, she streaked past Janelle and through the doors.

"Megan!"

Behind her, Megan heard the heavy tread of his footsteps, but they seemed to stop when he reached Janelle.

For an instant Megan was blinded by the brilliance of the lights in the ballroom and deafened by the noise after the dark quiet of the solarium. She could only stare at the glittering couples in bewilderment. She wanted to dance, to become part of the party and chatter vivaciously, to forget Jeb and all that he meant to her, all that she must never let him mean to her.

Oh, it wasn't fair to want someone and know she could never fit into his glittering circle of polished friends. Across the room she saw Nick. She wanted to run to him, but he was standing with Triple and Amy.

Nearby, Wayne Jackson was dancing with his wife. She wore a white gown and still moved as gracefully as a girl, having once been a prima ballerina. There were those who said they were the oddest of stormy mismatches—the Anglo-Texan rancher married to a cosmopolitan, world-class ballerina, living on land at the extremities of both their countries where the rivalry between the Mexican and Anglo cultures had never blended easily.

Wayne's silver-gold head bent low over his wife's dark one, and she gave him a radiant smile. Watching the intensity between them, Megan's heart ached with a bittersweet longing to know that kind of enduring love with a man.

Megan wandered through the house, seeking a quiet place where she could be alone. Kirk was in the drawing room, a beautiful blonde sitting beside him on the sofa.

"Union horses?" the girl murmured in disbelief. "In here?"

Megan heard the low rumble of Kirk's voice and knew that he was telling the girl the old story about how Union officers had ridden inside the house on horseback to kill Colonel Jackson, their horseshoes cutting deep half-moons into the wood. The colonel had escaped, but two of his vaqueros had been shot dead in the parlor.

Megan passed into the portrait gallery, where huge oil portraits lined the walls. All of the Jackson family was depicted there, even Jack, Jeb's younger wild brother who had been killed in a motorcycle accident. Even Julia. For a long moment Megan studied the painting of the little girl who had been her childhood playmate.

The painter had caught her intense charisma, although Julia had always been most beautiful when she was moving. Her face was a perfect oval, her eyes immense and as darkly luminous as black pearls. Her hair fell in thick waves to her shoulders. The tragedy of her kidnapping on that long-ago day had changed all of their lives. To have a child stolen, lost forever. Never to know if she were dead or alive...

It was said that Mercedes could never look at the painting without tears coming into her eyes. Having lost her own father, Megan could identify with Mercedes's pain.

Because it distracted her from her own misery, Megan studied the other pictures in the room. There were MacKay portraits alongside the Jackson ones, images of men in fringed leather jackets, men with long, wispy beards whose faces were carved with hard determination.

Megan knew the history of the two families by heart. Once the MacKays and Jacksons had been business partners. Together they had battled Indians and Mexican bandits. The Civil War had come and the soldiers who had protected the settlers from Indians were forced to abandon their forts and go to war. The frontier was pushed back a hundred miles, and had the ranchers not stood together, the MacKays and the Jacksons would have lost their fledgling empires.

Megan heard the sound of Kirk's crutches. His low voice came from behind her. She turned. He was alone.

"It's odd to think the MacKays were once richer and more powerful than the Jacksons," he said.

"I wish we still were."

"It's useless to cry for the moon, Megan," Kirk said gently. "When the land was tamed, the MacKays lost interest in it. They were adventurers, not ranchers."

You just think that because you happen to be an adventurer, she thought. Aloud she murmured, "Or maybe the Jacksons were just greedier."

"Or smarter," Jeb said, entering the room with Janelle on his arm. He stopped several feet away from Megan, bowing his head slightly, formally. Her heart began to beat loudly. "Don't look at me that way, Megan. I just said it because I know how you enjoy keeping all those old wounds open." He smiled boldly.

His deliberate cruelty stung. White-faced, Megan stared after him as he swept Janelle to the farthest corner of the room and began to talk about the famous paintings of the Alamo and San Jacinto as if they were the only two people in the room.

Watching them, Megan felt the bitter anguish of jealousy. She had come into the gallery to be alone. They were the last people she wanted to see. She must have betrayed something of her feelings because Kirk gave his sister a long quizzical look, but neither of them spoke.

"So this is where the party is," someone cried from the hallway.

Wayne and Mercedes entered the room along with several politicians and Jack Robards, the oilman who'd done all the drilling on the Jackson Ranch. Nick and Amy followed them in, Amy clutching Triple's hand tightly.

Mercedes inclined her dark head toward Megan, standing by Amy while Wayne lead the politicians down to a painting of Goliath, the finest bull the ranch had ever produced. The men talked of horses and bulls, of the ranch's money problems. Janelle and Jeb joined them. When Jack Robards turned the conversation to oil, expressing the hope that new exploration might help the ranch's cash flow, there was a moment of tension while everyone waited for Jeb's answer. Megan felt Jeb staring at her uneasily before he deftly changed the subject back to Goliath.

An inveterate matchmaker, Mercedes stared down the length of the gallery at her son. "Megan," she began in a soft undertone, "did you know this was my wedding picture?" Mercedes pointed to a portrait in front of Megan.

"You were very beautiful."

"All brides are beautiful—if they love the man they are marrying." Mercedes was watching Janelle and Jeb. "Janelle will make a beautiful bride before long."

"Yes…"

"I have always loved weddings and the birth of babies. They are the happiest times."

Megan could only nod.

"Have you seen the beautiful saddle Janelle gave Jeb for his birthday?"

"N-no."

"It's embroidered leather trimmed with sterling silver."

"How lovely."

Nick was kissing Amy tenderly. Triple had broken free of his mother's grasp and was gamboling back and forth in the long gallery like a lion cub on the prowl for mischief.

Mercedes sighed. "Every time I see Nick and Amy together I want the same thing for all our children. For Jeb, especially. I guess I worry about him the most because he went into ranching only to make Wayne and me happy. Jeb's always had such a strong sense of duty toward others that he neglects his own happiness. And lately...he's seemed so... I can't put my finger on it. I guess he's worried about our money problems. It's such a fight to hold onto a place like this. I keep remembering that Jeb wanted to be a doctor, that he even went to medical school before he was forced to take over the ranch. I'm afraid ranching alone will never satisfy him. Jeb needs the right woman to complete his life."

Mercedes was so absorbed in her thoughts that she

didn't notice the tall, dark figure standing behind them.

"And where does one find this paragon, Mother?"

Mercedes gave a quick, shaken little laugh. "Jeb, I didn't realize you were there."

He grinned at them both. "Obviously."

Janelle had remained with the other men beneath the painting of Goliath, and the conversation about cattle breeding had become more animated.

Mercedes couldn't meet her son's eyes. One of her hands toyed with the diamond necklace at her throat. "Dear, I was watching you with Janelle, and I couldn't help thinking…"

His eyes gleamed. He was studying Megan closely, looking into her eyes. "Janelle is indeed a paragon of charm and beauty. She will make the right man very happy," he murmured in a low voice.

Megan began to tremble slightly.

"I'm so glad you think so, dear."

"Will you both excuse me?" Megan whispered raggedly. "I—I'm not feeling very well. I…"

Jeb lifted his dark brows and watched her, hating the pain he saw in her eyes, the pain he had deliberately caused.

But he did not try to stop her as she ran from the room.

Nine

Megan fled down the stairs and into the balmy night. Shakily she clutched her purse and the gift she had meant to give Jeb, the bright paper torn from having been ripped out from under the pile of lavish presents.

Her first impulse when she'd left the party was to go home, but the sweetness of the Spanish guitar music and the cowboys' laughter floating on the night air made her turn toward the pool where the vaqueros were dancing. She needed the warmth and reassurance of their friendship. She wanted to forget Jeb's party, to forget Janelle's saddle, to forget how shabby her own gift to Jeb would have seemed in comparison.

Megan threw her purse and the gift down on a table where a single surviving candle in a hurricane glass was guttered low beside the waxen stumps of others that had gone out. She moved toward the music and the dance floor, her body swaying slightly to the rhythm of the strumming mariachis. In the soft light of the flickering lanterns, her skin was honey gold. Her hair swung loosely down her back like the softest flame.

A dozen velvet-black male eyes were riveted to her undulating form.

Lauro stepped out of the crowd of dark faces and asked her to dance a polka, and soon she was whirling around with everyone. The redolent scent of sizzling beef and onions being barbecued over an open mesquite fire wafted through the air. There was a piñata for the children. Some of the smaller children were playing pin-the-tail-on-the-burro. The older ones were dashing about in a game of tag that was quite lively— Triple had made his escape from Amy and was stealing tacks from the younger children and putting them to mischievous use. There were shrieks and yelps of laughter, the soft sounds of mothers' voices struggling to control their unruly children, and Triple's cries, wilder than all the others.

Megan danced until she was breathless, changing partners again and again, and almost forgetting her earlier unhappiness.

She was dancing with Tim Collins, amused that he

dared to tell her several of his favorite sexist jokes about female pilots. Like too many male flyers he considered women too emotional, vain, inconsistent and frivolous to fly airplanes. They were a hazard to others as well as themselves, he said. She was laughing at him, making a joke of his ridiculous views, when suddenly she became aware of a tall, dark man in formal evening clothes prowling restlessly along the edge of the dance floor.

Jeb...

Her laughter died in her throat.

"Bienvenidos."

"Welcome, Señor Jackson."

Jeb was greeted by his men and their wives as if he were one of them. They offered him beer and *fajitas*, and he took a beer, lifting it to his lips. Then he saw Megan and stopped dead where he was. Through narrowed black eyes he watched her.

Megan gaped at him, feeling like some disobedient schoolgirl caught in an escapade.

Tim whispered into her ear. "You're too pretty to fly. You should get married. Have children..."

She tossed her head defiantly and allowed herself to be spun around faster. Her green skirts were a gossamer pinwheel, whirling above her knees, revealing a blur of yellow petticoats and the slender grace of honey-gold legs.

Jeb bit his bottom lip and emitted a low growl as he threaded his way through the crowd toward her.

Megan's eyes widened as she realized his intent.

The dance floor was packed. Escape was impossible.

When he reached her, Jeb waved his brown hand in a swift, imperious gesture. The music stopped abruptly. A breathless, explosive hush fell upon the crowd.

He stood so close she could see every one of his thick eyelashes, every pore of his skin.

His glittering eyes surveyed her with a cool, cutting arrogance.

Not an ice cube tinkled. Even Triple was frozen.

Megan could feel her heart pounding, her legs turning to water.

Jeb's deep, low tone sliced through the silence. "May I cut in?"

Megan's green eyes blazed at him. She was the only one who could answer him. Tim had taken one look at Jeb and vanished.

"I said I want to dance with you," Jeb rasped.

Her gaze fell away from him. She felt exposed, vulnerable. He was making his interest in her plain, staking his claim like some primeval male. This was his territory. His eyes said: *this is my woman.*

Everyone stared at them with avid curiosity. For years there had been rumors. And now this.

Megan was blushing hotly. Tomorrow, and the next day afterward, and for all the days that followed, she would have to face these people.

She was furiously angry and a little frightened.

She stumbled back, but Jeb blocked her escape and drew her into his arms against his hard, muscled body. Her chest heaved against his. She could feel the heat of her body and the heat of his mingling. When she tried to twist away, his grip tightened gently.

The silence of the breathless crowd was like a crushing weight.

"I would be delighted to dance with you, *Mr. Jackson*," she murmured coolly, softly.

He smiled down at her, ignoring the hot brilliance of her eyes. He waved his hand lightly, signaling for the music, and she thought he'd never seemed more ruthless.

There were shouted bravos, applause, sighs of relief.

The guitars resumed, wilder, faster than before.

Brown fingers slid up the length of her honey-gold arm, and she shivered. She felt his other hand around her waist. Her own fingers rose slowly to his neck, stopping only when they brushed the silken, ink-dark tendrils that curled over his collar.

There was an unreal quality about the moment, a dreamlike magic that held them both in thrall. They stared into each other's eyes, he with heady triumph, she with a sensation of wild dismay.

He began to move, slowly at first, and she could do nothing but follow. Then the music took over and possessed them both. He was a superb dancer. He held her tightly, so tightly that her legs burned with the brush of his thighs, so tightly that her soft breasts felt the tiny hardness of his shirt studs. They danced as if their bodies were made to be together, to move together.

The song ended before it seemed to have begun. After it was over, they clung to each other in silence, their hearts pounding violently.

Everyone was changing partners. Megan came awake slowly as if from a dream and lifted her head dazedly from his shoulder, stunned by the primitive abandon he aroused in her. He was as arrogant and bullying as always. She tried to tell herself she would have run from him had he not been holding her fingers tightly, but that was a lie.

He lifted her hand to his lips and she felt the warmth of that gentle kiss between her fingers, tingling in every part of her body. When he released her hand slowly, she did not run away.

Megan looked up at him and saw mirrored in his black gaze the same powerful awareness of their physical closeness. His eyes blazed with something that was fierce and powerful, something she responded to without thought. No man had ever affected her like this. She felt weak at the knees, dizzy, completely his.

''I had forgotten it is the custom for a Jackson to make an appearance at the ranch hands' party,'' she said breathlessly, in an attempt to lighten the charged atmosphere between them.

"So had I." His eyes were deep and dark and still. "I came after you."

He was drawing her into his hard arms.

"Jeb—"

The music began again, and he whirled her across the dance floor, away from the other dancers and into the night darkness where they were soon utterly alone. Flat brush country stretched beneath an endless star-studded sky. There was a kind of peace in the emptiness of the land, an all-enveloping serenity in the vastness.

For a moment he held her in silence. She no longer tried to struggle as he sheltered her in his arms. Even though she knew she shouldn't, she let him bury his face in her hair. Nor could she stop herself from raising a hesitant hand and brushing his rough cheek with her fingertips.

The compelling spell of his virile masculinity was too strong. She wanted him, wanted to touch him, wanted to know again the indescribable ecstasy his finely muscled body could give her. The treacherous need was a torrent of fire flooding her veins.

"You left without even saying goodbye or happy birthday," he said gently.

"I didn't think you'd notice." Was that her own voice, soft as velvet, dying away in the darkness?

"I notice everything about you," he murmured.

Her fingertip stroked the length of his jaw. Warm sandpaper stretched over chiseled bone. He felt so hard and so hot, so very much a man.

Every part of her turned to jelly, uncertain, unsure.

"Happy birthday, then," she whispered. "There, are you happy now?"

He held her closer even than before, his hot, quick breath beating upon her ear.

"Only because you're in my arms," he whispered.

"Janelle is probably missing you."

"Janelle knows how to take care of herself," he muttered thickly.

"A commendable quality."

"She has lots of them." He was turning Megan's face up to his. "So do you."

"Oh, why don't you go back where you belong—with her?"

"Because I can't resist holding you in my arms." His voice was hoarse, a stranger's voice. His grip had tightened again. "Megan, Megan… Darling…" She felt his lips in her hair. "Forget Janelle. She doesn't matter anymore."

"I'm immune to your smooth lines," she said. Then why did she feel so thoroughly, so powerfully aroused?

"Are you?" He cupped her face in his warm hands. "I wonder." He brushed his thumbs lightly, lightly across the smooth curve of her cheekbones. "Megan, why did you run away tonight?"

There was an ache in the center of her being. "Because I don't fit into your world. Because...I can't, ever. I'm not like your mother or Janelle. I can't give parties—"

"They can't fly airplanes or lead secret commando missions into Mexico," he said softly, tenderly. "Besides, you were the most beautiful woman there."

"My dress was too loud. My hair..."

"It suits you."

"Everybody kept looking at me."

His gaze strayed to her mouth, and he watched her tongue flick around the edges, moistening it. Her head was thrown back, her eyes half-closed. Her racing pulse throbbed in her throat.

The sight of her made his own heart pound swiftly. He drew a deep breath. "You were meant to stand out. To be looked at."

He unpinned the golden rose from his lapel and tucked it into her hair. "There." He bent his dark head, and his lips slanted against her temple in a feather-light kiss. "I've wanted to do that all night. You were meant to wear flowers in your hair. I couldn't take my eyes off you."

"That's why I left."

"Why?" The single word was thick with passion.

"Because you were there," she said tremulously. "Because you kept following me. Because every time I saw you I couldn't forget that one night of madness, of weakness."

He smiled faintly. "So you admit that it was unforgettable."

"You are a rogue, a devil."

"Because I don't deny that I want you." He smiled. "There are women who find such men attractive."

"Not me."

"You seemed to—that once."

"I'm an employee and you're my boss, in case you've forgotten."

"You're more than that now." His lips touched her on her brow. "Much more."

"So you keep telling me. What happened never should have happened."

"But I can't forget it. I don't even want to."

"I want to."

"Do you?" His mouth was very near hers. "You have a magic for me that no other woman has ever had. I couldn't feel so much for you if you felt nothing for me."

"You belong with a woman in pearls or diamonds and designer gowns."

"Promise me you'll never wear pearls...or diamonds or designer gowns." He chuckled. His hand smoothed back a silken tangle of russet hair. "Not till you're quite old—at least thirty-four. Until then, I want you just as you are now—in soft green dresses with flowers in your hair. In blue jeans. In Piper Cubs."

She stared at him. His black hair waved down over his brown forehead, and his eyes shone darkly with some intense emotion. Shaken, she murmured a wordless reply.

There was only the wild throb of the music, the thick, softly scented warmth of the darkness. He lifted her arms and looped them around his neck. At his molding of her body against his, a wild tremor raced along her nerves. Her skin burned as though touched by fire.

His hands tightened on her waist, and Megan felt another tremulous wave of longing course through her body.

His mouth nuzzled into the hot pulse beat near her collarbone, and she shuddered with some new yet anciently vital desire.

His hand slid down her spine. She held her breath, her skin tingling with need and anticipation.

His mouth was a hard, sensual line that beckoned her excitingly.

"Kiss me," she murmured soundlessly. But he didn't. He continued stroking her slowly, rhythmically.

She could no longer resist the temptation of his mouth, and finally an unbearable wave of sensuality made her lean up and kiss him.

Her mouth was soft, hot satin sliding against his. She felt the sudden harsh rasp of his breathing as his tongue slid inside. His mouth slanted demandingly across hers, filling her everywhere with a melting, tingling warmth.

His arms crushed her against him. The breath caught in her throat, and she pressed her body into his. He made a faint groaning sound, then combed his fingers through the long, thick spirals of flame that spilled everywhere. His mouth left her mouth, and he pressed little kisses everywhere, kissing her earlobe, her throat, softly at first and then with a swift gradation of intensity that made her tremble.

Something raw and elemental leapt between the contact of hard male lips and velvety female flesh. She stood motionless under his caresses, sighing in dizzying surrender until at last he pulled away.

"I love you," she whispered, clinging to him.

She caught a glimpse of his face as he exhaled a deep breath of shock. His eyes were wide and brilliant with some emotion that terrified her.

It was then that she realized the horror of what she had admitted.

"I knew you felt it, too." His voice was hoarse with triumph.

She let him go. "Yes, I feel it," she moaned. "I feel it, and it's making me miserable."

"Why?"

"Because I was happier hating you. Don't you understand? I know you. You drove my father away."

"You're wrong about that," he said quietly.

"All you've ever wanted is land and money and

power, and you'll do anything and use anybody to get them. You chose your first wife because she was rich. Because she was the kind of woman Jacksons marry. You need money now, so you'll marry for it again."

"Those are lies, Megan. Everybody else in your life walked out on you, so you can't trust anybody."

"I know you, Jeb, and because I know you, I don't want to feel anything for you. A long time ago I looked up to you. I trusted you and loved you, and you betrayed that love. You took everything from me that mattered. Everything—my father, my self-respect. I can't let that happen a second time. All I want now is to be your employee. Nothing more."

"I don't believe you."

She backed away, her eyes shimmering with unshed tears. "Oh, please, please just leave me alone. Go back to Janelle."

Rage and other emotions she didn't understand flamed in his dark eyes. "I don't think that's really what you want."

"It is!"

Jeb stood in silence, his features haggard, with new lines biting deeply into his face. He was filled with frustration and fury and injured feelings. He did not trust himself to speak. Those were the emotions she'd aroused in him for years. But he felt something else, too, something he no more welcomed than she: a keen need for her that was growing deeper every day.

As Megan ran through the brush in the darkness,

her gown snagged on something. He heard the sound of fabric shredding, her startled cry of dismay.

He took a step toward her to help her. Then he remembered her scathing words, and the memory cut him to the quick. She'd said she didn't want him.

If only he could erase her from his mind, from his heart, as easily.

He reached into his pocket and shook a cigarette into his hand. His lighter snapped, and he bent his head, inhaling deeply. He stood in the darkness, smoking, trying to contemplate a life with the proper sort of moneyed wife, a life without Megan.

He thought of never touching her, of never tilting her face to his, of never tasting her lips again, of never pressing her hot, naked body beneath his, and it was hell.

He threw his cigarette to the ground and crushed it with his heel. He needed to get drunk, to find a willing woman and forget.

He strode back to the party and was immediately aware of the vaqueros watching him as he poured himself a whiskey. A dozen pairs of eyes were glued to him as he downed it in a single draft. He knew he looked drawn and tired, his face stamped with anguish and rage, but there wasn't a damned thing he could do about it. The vaqueros were silent, their eyes curious, accusing, as he lifted the bottle and poured a second. He wanted to snarl at them to stop staring at him like that. Doubtless they had seen Megan and taken note of her tumbled hair and her torn dress and thought he had abused her in some way. By tomorrow it would be all over the county.

Suddenly he slammed his glass onto the nearest table so hard that the whiskey sloshed onto his fingers, onto the cloth, staining it.

It was no good drinking to forget. No good taking another woman because the one he wanted wouldn't have him.

Without a word he left the party. But he was aware of the silent eyes, everywhere, watching him, judging him.

On his way out of the party, he stumbled against a darkened table. His fingers clamped around the edge and he lifted it off its legs. He felt like hurling it into the darkness. Then the sight of his own name, clumsily scrawled across a rumpled red package, arrested him. Instantly he recognized Megan's handwriting, as well as her sparkling emerald-green clutch lying forgotten beside the gift.

The sharp breath he took cut into his chest like a knife. He should go on to the house. It didn't mean anything—her bringing him a gift. Slowly he set the table down and picked the package up, all the while cursing himself for the flicker of hope he felt. He carefully peeled the paper away.

Incredibly his fingers touched something smooth and wooden. He pulled out the carved figure he had wanted for years, staring at it in numb amazement.

Jeb clutched the carving, turning it over so that it gleamed in the muted light of the flickering candle. He remembered that day, so long ago, when she'd loved him, when she'd kissed him, when he'd picked flowers for her and she'd worn them in her hair. She'd offered herself freely to him.

His fingers tightened convulsively around the figure. A smile crept across his dark face, its light softening his hard black eyes.

"Well, I'll be damned," he whispered.

He would make her come to him again and offer herself to him again, if it was the last thing he ever did!

But how?

What method of gentle persuasion did a man use on a woman as stubborn and hardheaded as Megan MacKay?

Ten

"Jeb! Oh, dear God! Help!"

Megan was caught in a cage of fire. Tree trunks were wavering bars of flame. Vaguely she was aware of some alien sound screaming in the distance as she collapsed on the forest floor.

In that final precious moment, she knew that more than anything she wanted to live. To love. She wanted Jeb, and she was filled with an overwhelming sadness that she would die and he would never know.

She was being sucked down a blinding tunnel of fire.

Megan bolted awake and sprang out of bed, gasping. It was her old nightmare, the same as always, yet different.

Her nightgown was soaked with sweat. The unvarnished floor stung like dry ice against her bare toes, but in that first, awful moment, she was just grateful to be alive. She sank down onto her bed, weak with relief and with a new terrible sensation of loneliness.

The sound from her nightmare jangled, and she realized it was the telephone by her bed.

The room was as black as death.

The phone erupted again, and she jumped.

Who...

Terrified, she groped for the phone, only to send it crashing to the floor. She pulled it up by the cord.

"Hello," she murmured breathlessly, shakily.

"What took you so long?" drawled an insolent male tone.

"Jeb?"

Her heart quickened. An ache rose in her to be held in his strong arms, to be crushed against his broad chest, to know all the tenderness she'd always longed for and never had, and yet there was a new jeering quality in his voice that made her wary.

He laughed softly, ironically. "Who else would call you at this hour?"

"What time..." She felt bewildered, out of her depth as she fumbled in the dark for her lamp chain.

"What does it matter?" he asked derisively. "I'm the boss. You're the employee—one of many."

There was a difference in his tone, and it made her shiver. "What do you want?" she whispered.

"Janelle needs to go home first thing in the morning. Have the jet ready around ten. I don't want her kept waiting."

Janelle... The tender core inside Megan froze, and she listened to him uncomprehendingly. Janelle. Megan's fingers found the chain to her lamp and yanked.

She read her watch, and she could feel the bitter coldness in her heart spreading. "Who do you think you are, calling me at 4:00 a.m.?"

"Your boss, honey."

Anger churned her stomach as she suddenly realized what he was doing. He was getting even.

"Jeb, I didn't mean..."

"Do you think I give a damn what you meant or didn't mean? From now on you'll do as I say. Or quit. This was your idea, remember?" His low, hard voice went on. "I want the plane serviced and immaculate. Arrange for coffee and light snacks to be brought on board. Make sure everything's hot. I'll expect a full briefing on the weather. I want to stop in Phoenix and take Janelle to lunch there at a favorite restaurant of hers."

Megan clenched the receiver in a death grip and imagined it was his dark, brown throat. But it wasn't, and the smooth, quiet voice continued, making demand after demand, every one of them a gratuitous insult in some way, until all the residual tenderness she'd felt toward him after her dream was gone. She was shaking and limp with fury.

"I'm not some servant you can call up and order around at any hour of the day or night!"

"Read the fine print of your contract and you'll discover that's exactly what you are," he purred. "It's what you said you wanted to be, remember?"

At last he hung up, finally drawling softly, "Sweet dreams!"

In her hands the jet was metal made living flesh; a diamond point scratching the sky.

Megan studied the ominous tranquillity of the arid mesas and sheer rock peaks stretching out twenty thousand feet beneath her with an odd feeling of misgiving. Normally she loved flying; she loved the spaciousness of the sky; she loved the lonely peace high above the rumpled carpet of hills and valleys and mountains.

But today a vague uneasiness disturbed her.

The weather forecast had been acceptable—clear skies until the Pacific coast, and only isolated or widely scattered moderate rain showers and thunderstorms there. There were no sigmets or other severe weather advisories issued, but she instinctively grasped the controls tightly. Something she didn't understand tightened every muscle in her body as though she were bracing herself for danger. Time and again she forced herself to relax; she reminded herself that this odd foreboding was probably nothing more than the tension of Jeb and Janelle's presence in the cabin behind her.

Megan had been furious at Jeb ever since his pre-dawn phone call. Her anger had intensified when he arrived at the jet two hours late, deliberately, thoughtlessly having kept her waiting. He had strutted to the plane with Janelle's hand laced tightly through his, and grinning cockily down at Megan, he had ordered her to take off immediately, saying that they were in a hurry and didn't want to be kept waiting.

Megan had swallowed her burning fury, crawled into the cockpit and prepared for takeoff. They were now over New Mexico.

Behind her, Megan heard the door open and close, and involuntarily her fingers tightened on the controls. Jeb sprawled in the seat beside her, staring at her. Bold, dark eyes swept over her, and every muscle in her body buzzed in response.

"I just came up to say that you're flying my Lear jet, not some pickup truck on a bumpy ranch road. You're scaring the hell out of Janelle!"

"I know perfectly well I'm not flying a pick—" Megan's voice cracked.

He was grinning, smirking with triumph.

He was trying to make her mad and she knew it.

Her cheeks flushed with anger. She had never hated anyone so much in her entire life.

"The food was cold!" he said cheerily.

"Because you were late!"

"A good employee—"

His arrogance was like a spark set to dynamite.

"Why don't you go back to the cabin and torture Janelle?"

"Janelle doesn't call being with me torture," he taunted in his silken, amused tone.

"Whatever she calls it, why don't you just leave?"

His devilish grin flashed in her direction. "Because it's more fun being up here."

He touched Megan's shoulder, and she felt a shock go through her whole body. It was like electricity. It burned them both.

She saw that his eyes were blazing. He felt it, too.

"Megan," he rasped, more softly than he'd ever spoken to her. "It doesn't have to be this—"

She felt a treacherous softening at the center of her being. "Just go," she said with a look that glazed the warmth in his eyes with a layer of ice.

When he spoke, his voice was bitter and cold. "I will in a minute. But first, try to make a gentle landing in Phoenix. For once."

What was he trying to do, make her so mad she flew his plane straight into the ground?

She sat there staring ahead into the deep, shimmering blue, her hands clenched rigidly on the controls. Megan sucked in her bottom lip and bit it until it bled.

In Phoenix they were on the ground for four hours. Jeb didn't like her landing and told her so in a cool,

disdainful tone, right in front of Janelle, and Megan
smoldered with ill-suppressed fury. Then he ordered
Megan to stay with the jet while he and Janelle drove
into town. Megan paced back and forth, drinking cup
after cup of cold, stale tea while she waited, inter-
rupting this pastime every so often to thumb through
a dog-eared aviation magazine or to listen to another
weather report. But all she could do was fume as she
thought of Jeb and his new perplexing determination
to keep her in this constant state of rage.

When Jeb returned from lunch, he ignored Megan
completely, and somehow that was even worse than
his rudeness. Every time he looked at Janelle, Megan
felt an emptiness echoing through her soul.

When they took off again, the flight was uneventful
at first. But as they neared California, a thick wall of
cloud began to push up over the mountains. Megan
talked to a controller and he gave her the latest
weather, which didn't sound nearly as ominous as
things were beginning to look.

By the time Megan was setting up her approach for
the strip near the Jacobs's ranch, monstrous cumulus
clouds were puffed up on all sides of them, boxing
them in. Somewhere at the base of those clouds, lost
in the murk and rain, were the razor-sharp mountains
of the Santa Lucia Range. And the strip.

The news from the radio began to sound less reassuring. In the space of ten minutes a monstrous system of thunderstorms had sprung to life and grown

with astonishing intensity around them. She talked back and forth to the controller only to learn that the weather at the nearest alternate airports was no better.

They were trapped.

Megan was tired, too tired for this life-and-death emergency. She hadn't gotten enough sleep, and Jeb's harassment had wearied her. Fatigue gnawed at her, numbing her mind and sapping her strength. She shifted in her seat, trying to find a more comfortable position.

An extraordinary violet-red thunderhead towered menacingly in front of her, higher than all the rest.

Hell.

Megan flashed on the seat-belt sign, and Jeb came into the cabin. "What's the matter?"

"Over there," she pointed. "We've got to land in this."

The setting sun had tinged the curling bellies of the huge clouds brilliantly iridescent shades of pink and lavender.

"All I see is pretty clouds."

"They're gorgeous...but deadly. The winds inside them can tear this plane to pieces in seconds."

"It's your job to prevent that." Jeb buckled himself in beside her. "The question is can you?"

She let go of the controls.

The jet dropped two hundred feet in one second.

"Easy," Jeb murmured.

She didn't trust herself to speak. Not that she

needed to. He would get his. And soon. There wasn't a Jackson alive who had the stomach for flying when things really got rocky. Even though Jeb was a licensed pilot, and a good one, she knew he'd only learned to fly as a safety precaution. With some satisfaction she noted the extreme pallor of his chiseled features as the winds caught the plane and tried to fling it across the sky.

"If you had an ounce of sense, you'd choose a better time to harass me," she whispered, gripping the controls. "There are mountains down there, and our ceiling's so low, we can't see them."

He shut up. She noted that his fingers were locked around the armrests like iron manacles. But she knew he was ready to help her if she needed it.

The clouds billowed up on all sides of the jet like giant beasts filled with dark potency. The plane hurtled down, into the clouds. Soon there was nothing outside the windows but cold, gray nothingness. Rain began to batter the windshield, and she had only her instruments to guide her, only the tense disembodied voice of the controller.

"Jacobs Tower to Lear 2835 Tango. We have you on radar. We're going to bring you in. Turn two degrees east and descend four thousand feet. At your present airspeed, you should be down in ten minutes."

She forgot Jeb and focused her complete attention on flying, using every skill she had ever acquired.

Down, down. She watched the glide slope needle overshoot the center mark, drift back up and stop near the middle as she finally got the descent rate stabilized. Then the plane was hammered on three sides by violent winds. The jet rolled to the right, abruptly, and then plunged under the belly of a cloud.

Megan stole a quick glance at the altimeter. The needle was edging below forty-five hundred feet. That was a lot of altitude in flat Texas ranch country, but over Big Sur... She could almost feel the mountains rushing up to meet them.

Beads of perspiration popped out on her brow. Her hands were so clammy they stuck to the controls.

"Jacobs Tower to Lear 2835 Tango. Descend to thirty-five hundred feet and maintain."

Down. Down. Did this pea-soup visibility go clear to the ground?

Thirty-five hundred feet, and she broke out of the clouds just in time to see deadly, sharp rock looming up with alarming suddenness, rising less than fifty feet below the jet.

Another second in the clouds and they would all have been dead.

She heard Jeb's low, guttural curse as she banked instinctively to evade the wall of rock.

The jet careened like the wildest roller coaster car. Jeb's features were drawn tautly across his cheekbones; his dark skin blanched by fear.

Suddenly, through the rain, she saw the flat, hard

glimmer of the ocean, the white waves crashing into the headlands, the green rolling hills of the Jacobs's ranch and the dark straight gash that was the landing strip.

"We're going to make it," she whispered.

Jeb didn't look at her, didn't speak.

Three minutes later the jet was on the ground, taxiing to the hangar. When she brought it to a stop, Megan switched off the engines with numb fingers and sat rigidly still, hardly able to breathe.

There was a heavy silence inside the jet. Outside, corrugated tin doors were rumbling and scraping closed in their concrete tracks. Rain was slashing down as the men rushed up to help them out.

Jeb unclenched his hands from the armrest. She heard the metallic unsnapping of his buckle. Without a word, he got up and left her.

Not one word to her for having gotten them down. Being a pilot himself, he had to know what a miracle that landing had been. It was as if she meant nothing.

From the cabin she heard Jeb's voice, speaking softly, soothingly to Janelle. "She scared the hell out of me, too, honey. Don't worry, I'll give her a talking to later that she won't forget, but only after I get you home and make sure you're all right."

Not one word to indicate he might have cared that Megan was scared, too.

Her face was as still as petrified wood.

She heard the hatch open, their retreating steps and Jeb's softest, solicitous drawl.

Something inside her exploded.

He had not bothered to send a car back for her! Megan's heart was near bursting as she threw herself inside the silent, dark house. Consumed by the wildest, the most gut-tearing emotion she'd ever known, she closed the door and sagged against it, white-faced, wild-eyed and panting, like some tormented character from a melodrama. Her hands were shaking, her teeth chattering. She was sopping wet and every part of her body felt frozen. Behind the door, the storm still raged.

He had not sent the car back for her even after she'd called him on the phone! A spasm of nausea boiled up in her throat, and she pressed a hand weakly to her mouth. The awful feeling subsided, but it left her even weaker than before.

Because of Jeb she'd fought her way through that storm. Because of him she was shivering and frozen, queasy with starvation.

At last she caught her breath, and the mad hammering of her heart slowed. At last she regained enough strength to stumble through the hushed stillness of the vast, cavernous rooms of the Jacobs's Big Sur ranch house to Jeb's room.

It was past midnight. Having forgotten her, everyone had gone to bed, and she'd had to let herself in.

She had shouted, but the hollow echoes of her own voice had been her only answer. She could have died, and no one would have stirred.

As she made her way across the living room, she left a trail of puddles and oozing mud on the Saltillo tiles and priceless Oriental throw rugs, but she was too filled with rage to care.

Nothing mattered but finding Jeb.

He had treated her as though she were less than nothing! He had driven away with Janelle and left Megan alone at the strip, not caring that she'd been as terrified as he, not caring that she hadn't slept or eaten, not bothering to send a driver for her even after she'd phoned him.

In the end, too proud to call him again or to let the others at the hangar know of his humiliating treatment of her, she'd walked the quarter mile between the strip and the house in a freezing, bone-chilling downpour.

She stumbled past the kitchen and the hall that led to the little room in the back that she was always given when Jeb flew to the Jacobs's. Stiff, wet leather boot tops were cutting into her ankles. She stopped, unlaced her boots, and threw them aside. Then she ran barefoot up the wide staircase and down the long corridors to Jeb's room. She knocked urgently, breathlessly against the cool, wooden door, all the time hating herself for how she had let him treat her.

Maybe he was going to marry Janelle, but he was

never, never going to walk all over Megan MacKay again.

When he didn't answer, she twisted the knob and stepped into his large bedroom. She stood there a moment, uncertain, dripping on the plush thickness of the wine-red carpet.

The long windows beside his bed were open, and rain was blowing inside. For a second she wondered how he could have slept through her shouts.

White curtains billowed eerily. Thrown across the sofa were his suitcase and clothes. The temperature was like ice, and her teeth and jaws began to rattle.

"J-Jeb..."

There was no answer from the silent, snugly ensconced lump in the middle of that immense bed.

She moved closer and whispered his name a second time, and again there was only the blowing wind and the endless silence of the house falling around her like an icy cloak.

She knelt closer to him, saw his shiny black hair, and detected the faint steady rhythm of his breathing. Droplets of water ran from her hair, spattered the smooth white sheets and ran down his brown neck. She drew back, then she caught herself as she realized what she was doing.

Why was she creeping silently into his room? Being thoughtful of his comfort when he hadn't given a damn for hers? He'd been sound asleep in the warm comfort of his bed while she'd been stumbling through mud and rain!

In a frenzy of uncontrollable wrath, she snatched the corners of his bedspread, his blankets, his sheets, everything on the bed, and yanked.

His hand snaked out of the darkness and clamped around her wrist.

Soft, dripping-wet woman-skin was snapped tightly against the rock-hard, molten heat of man.

He hadn't been asleep at all.

"What took you so long?" he murmured huskily, his warm breath fluttering against the mad pounding at her throat.

His lazy, amused voice was like gasoline deliberately thrown on the flaming coals of her rage.

For some inexplicable reason, he wanted her mad.

Every cell in her being ignited with anger.

"I've been waiting for you for hours," he whispered.

She scarcely heard him.

In that first split second of blinding fury she didn't register that he was nude.

When she did, it was already too late.

He towered over her, naked, erect, magnificent.

A wild scream of rage bubbled up in her throat as she lunged forward, seeking to strike him, but he swung her off her feet into his arms. His mouth came down over hers, his lips hard and hot and demanding, his tongue filling her, his muscled body shuddering against the cold wetness of her skin. The moment he touched her, she belonged to him utterly.

The wind howled. Outside, lightning spattered an ink-black sky. Thunder rumbled. Man and woman were at the center of the wildness.

A storm of exquisite sensation radiated from his flesh to hers. Her skin was like ice, but the center of her became fire. Incredulously the wildness of her anger was transformed into violent, insatiable, carnal hunger. She was gasping for breath, murmuring his name, straining her body into his.

Weakly her hands circled his neck, her fingernails digging into his brown skin. She had come to him, hating him; then his burning mouth had touched hers, possessed hers, and she discovered that her all-consuming hatred was hopelessly entangled in an all-consuming love. He had taken her into his arms, molded her to the rigid heat of his body, and proved she had never belonged anywhere else. As his mouth played across hers, all her hatred and pain and loneliness were destroyed by a flood of desire that flowed from him into every cell of her body.

One kiss and his mouth set her body aflame.

Time stood still.

And she knew that until this night she had never known herself. She had thought she hated him, but she'd never hated him at all. She had thought she could deny her love only to discover she could deny him nothing.

His hands moved over her body, warming her, touching her intimately, and she knew the pattern of her life had been changed forever.

Without a word he pulled her down to the bed. She lay beneath him, her eyes ablaze through her dense, half-lowered lashes, and let him strip her. She felt the feverish urgency of his hot trembling hands ripping the buttons from her wet blouse; she felt those rough, callused fingers brushing against her nipples as he peeled away the gauzy, soaked shirt that had glued itself to her damp skin. His quick, naked urgency was hers.

Megan was no longer herself. She was some new, vitally alive being.

"I want you," she whispered. "Now... Please, I can't wait."

His husky, desire-tinged laughter teased her from the darkness. Outside the sky flashed fire, and the rain fell in torrents.

He made her wait, deliberately tantalizing her senses as he ran a single callus-tipped finger from her lips, over her chin, down her throat, down the satiny skin between her breasts, dipping into her navel and finally moving between her thighs into the soft womanliness of her. She lay on the bed quivering helplessly beneath his velvet touch, waiting, wanting him, dying for him as an erotic tide of tingling excitement inundated her senses.

His thighs pressed between hers. He lowered his

molten body. Naked flesh slid against naked flesh. Hard bronzed maleness into honey-gold woman. Fury fusing with desire, forever, irrevocably into love. Waves of passion, savage in their intensity, left her sighing, gasping, clinging, crying out his name again and again.

Man and woman came together in a wanton, torrid, soul-destroying splendor.

The bedroom was filled with the cool, sweet smell of spring rain, of the salty scent of sea air rolling in over the emerald hills, of the musky odor of love-making.

Years of loneliness fell away from her.

She could not get enough of him.

Megan came awake slowly, and the world was new. It was a beautiful morning—damp and fresh and cold. Water droplets glistened with the fiery jewel colors of the dawn through the green foliage that dripped outside the open window. A bird was singing a love song.

Beside her Jeb slept. His black head lay against her pale shoulder, his hushed breathing tickling the skin beneath her ear. Beneath the covers, nestled against her, his muscled body felt toasty warm, and she did not dare stir for fear of waking him. In those first moments she felt no guilt. Her pleasure and satiation were too complete; she had craved him for too long.

Vaguely she remembered her father and Jeb's driving him away. She had promised herself she would hate Jeb forever for that, but strangely, the hatred was gone. She only felt drained, depleted and utterly contented.

She shut her eyes languorously and drifted to sleep again. When she awakened a second time, she felt the weight of his massive upper body across hers. He was staring down at her, his eyes ablaze in his arrogant, handsome face. One of his fingers caressed her throat.

She should have been mortified, but she liked lying under him this way and felt a glow from the shivery excitement that radiated along her nerve endings at every point where his body touched hers. She liked the way his fingers trailed lightly across her hot skin, and she smiled drowsily at him.

He smiled back, the warmth of his feelings in his eyes. "It's late," he whispered lovingly, lowering his mouth to her throat and kissing her gently. "You'd better go back to your room before the Jacobses find you here."

At first the meaning of his words were lost to her. All she was conscious of was his mouth against her flesh. His kisses, passing from her throat to her breast where his teeth made little nibbles, sent spasms of pleasure down her spine.

"Honey, you'd better go," he murmured, withdrawing his lips.

Drowsily she opened her torpid eyes and became slowly aware of his impatience to be rid of her.

Quite suddenly, like sunlight leaving the day, the joy went from her heart. He wanted her gone! He didn't want anyone to know he'd slept with her! She had given herself to him desperately, completely, irrevocably, and she had never considered the experience might have been no more than a casual diversion for him.

"Why, y-you don't want people knowing you slept with me," she gasped, pulling away, trying to stifle her hurt.

His hot, dark gaze swept her possessively. He dragged her back beneath his body, and his sensuous fingers stroked her breast. "Is it so wrong—not wanting to share this, to share you with the world?" he asked in a soft, low tone.

She felt paralyzed. All her life she had wanted desperately to be loved. She had lost her mother, and her father, too. Last night she had thrown herself into the arms of the one man who had helped take these things from her.

Suddenly she was filled with self-disgust that made her stomach wrench into a tight knot of pain. Last night she'd made a passionate, daring bid for momentary happiness, only to awaken to the cold reality of a man who would never do anything but use her. It was because of Janelle that Jeb was so anxious to send her away.

Megan glanced at his black head, her conflicting

feelings tearing at her. She wanted to hate him, but she knew she could never hate him again.

He did not see her tragic expression. With infinite sweetness his mouth took the pink, hardened tip of her breast and lightly let his tongue play across it.

"It's because of Janelle," Megan insisted in a tear-choked voice, "isn't it—that you want me gone?"

He caught the throb of agony in her tone.

"Darling," he murmured very gently as his arms wrapped around her more tightly. He lifted his dark handsome face and saw the terrible hurt in her eyes. "No, darling, it's only you I'm thinking of. Please believe me."

"I—I don't understand," she whispered.

"It's your reputation I'm worried about. Not Janelle's. How could you think…"

Megan stared at him in disbelief. "Why would you care about that?"

Very slowly, very carefully, he cupped her face in his hands and held it still. "Because I don't want there to be any gossip about my future wife."

In his eyes she saw a violence of emotion as powerful as her own.

Megan's heart lurched in a pounding rush. "W-what?"

"I'm asking you to marry me."

He bent his head and kissed her lips, suckling them until a moan escaped her.

"Jeb," she began, at a loss.

His mouth was nuzzling her lips. His nose nuzzled her nose. "I want you, Megan, more than I've ever wanted any woman. It's as simple as that."

Nothing between them had ever been simple.

"I was so sure you'd only consider a woman with money or oil."

His face darkened. "You were wrong."

"But we fight all the time."

He laughed softly. "Not all the time." His breath fell hotly against her cheek. "I think we've discovered a new, mutually enjoyable sport."

She blushed shyly, aware of a thrilling happiness. "We can't spend our whole life in bed."

"Then we can spend our days looking forward to the nights."

"Sex is only a small part of marriage," she persisted.

"But an interesting part."

"I've hated you for years. I've blamed you for so many of the things that went wrong in my life. I'm not sure I can ever fit into your world."

"Honey, you're already a part of my world. We grew up together. We love the same things, the same people. We desire each other. People have begun marriages on less."

"Jeb, listen—"

"No, you listen. I can't wait." When he lowered his mouth to hers again, he was shaking. A long time later, against her lips, he muttered hoarsely, "I want you, and I intend to have you from now on, whether or not you marry me. I'm willing to settle for less than marriage, but I don't intend to do without you." His mouth grazed hers again. "Do you really think you can say no to me forever?" He laughed softly as he pulled her unresisting body against his own.

Everywhere her skin touched his, she felt on fire. "Even if I were crazy enough to agree," she began breathlessly, "that wouldn't mean I'd let you order me around the way you do everybody else on the ranch, the way you were ordering me around yesterday."

He grinned. "That's beginning to sound like a yes." His voice was low, soft. "But I'm not about to go down in history as the first Jackson who let his woman boss him."

"What kind of marriage can we possibly have?"

"It won't ever be dull."

"What about Janelle? Yesterday…"

"I already broke up with her. In Texas."

"You mean you deliberately made me think that you were still serious about her? You had me fly her here. You treated me like I was nothing."

"When I found your gift on the table Saturday night, I knew you loved me, but you'd said you wanted to be nothing more than an employee. Don't you see? I had to show you how wrong you were. It was a gamble, but I could see conventional methods of courting weren't working with you."

"You mean yesterday was nothing more than an unconventional method of courtship?" she cried.

"Call it what you like. I had to get you good and mad, so mad you couldn't think straight. You're more honest emotionally when you're furious. I had to get you back in my bedroom so you would know, as I do, that we belong together. Darling, you brought all this on yourself by being so stubborn."

"Me? You're the one who can't take no for an answer. You're the one who drove off and left me! You made me walk through that storm!"

"Then you'd better marry me, Megan. For both our sakes. If you don't, there's no telling what I'll do next." He kissed her then with tenderness and pulled her beneath him. "Because I will never, never let you go," he whispered.

Eleven

A solitary tear traced a sparkling trail down the smoothness of Megan's pale cheek as she moved through the tall wet bluestem. Beyond the hangar her little yellow airplane seemed to wait for her in the still quiet.

If only her father would come home, she thought, she might be deliriously happy. During the past week she had known endless, enchanted hours filled with undreamed-of rapture in Jeb's arms. Despite the rushed chaos of their wedding plans, for entire days they had existed only for each other, wanted only each other, celebrated only in each other.

It was a fine Texas dawn with a blood-red sun and

a humid fresh wind stirring the grasses in the pastures and the oak and emerald-dark ebony leaves. Morning, sun and the fresh wind brought with them earthy livestock smells as well as the dewy sweetness of mesquite and wildflowers.

There was a sense of vastness, of eternity, of quiet and peace. A sense of all her yesterdays, of all her tomorrows. A sense of belonging.

Megan craved these things. They were her world, the only security she had ever known.

It was the morning of her wedding day, and she was to marry the man she wanted above all others. Yet her heart was near to bursting with pain. She stared out at the vast emptiness. On such a morning as this one her father had disappeared from the ranch forever. And when he'd gone, he'd taken with him his daughter's belief in herself and in love.

A strange aching hollowness seemed to lodge in the pit of her stomach as she remembered that day, when she'd been forced to set aside all her childish illusions. There was a part of her that still felt lost and abandoned. Some part of her that was guilty because he hadn't loved her enough to stay. She wanted him back. She wanted to know why he had left her, what she had done wrong. And she had never wanted him more than today, this, the most special day of her life—not even on that first quiet morning so long ago.

Was he dead or alive? Would she ever know?

Had he loved her at all?

If he had, oh, what had she done, dear God, that was awful enough to drive him away?

If he didn't come home today, she would have to accept, once and forever, that he was never coming back.

Kirk was no comfort. He said only, "Dad went away for good. Accept it."

When she had confided in Jeb how much she wanted her father to be at her wedding, Jeb had nodded gravely. She had been surprised at the deep, tortured understanding she'd read in his eyes. He'd tackled the problem with grim resolve, placing full-page ads in all the important Texas newspapers and in several national ones. When the week had passed, and there'd been no response, Jeb had held her close and told her she had to accept the fact that Glen was either dead or didn't want to come.

She'd wept bitterly against Jeb's broad chest, saying that she knew now for sure that her father was dead, that she knew it because he would never have failed to come home for their wedding if he were alive. He could not have read the pleading letter published in all of those papers and still not come home. Jeb's mood had become even darker than her own. He'd torn free of her clinging arms, almost pushed her away, and gone off by himself, not returning until late last night.

She'd been frantic about Jeb then, and a terrible desolation had filled her soul. Everyone who'd ever loved her had abandoned her. When he'd come back, she'd made him promise gravely he would never leave her again without telling her where he was going.

But would he, too, walk out on her one day? Jeb... Was the fire between them true love? Or was it the darker, mutually destructive emotion she'd always believed it to be?

The Jacksons had been shocked by the news of the wedding, but they had struggled to camouflage their disappointment in Jeb's choice of bride by pretending it was the suddenness of the event that bothered them. Mercedes had nearly fainted when Jeb had first told her.

"One week to plan the biggest, grandest wedding in Texas. No one will come," Mercedes had protested. "The house..."

"Forget the house, Mother. Forget big and grand. Megan and I don't care if anyone comes."

Jeb had drawn his bride into his arms and kissed her with a tenderness and gentleness that had finally succeeded in touching his mother's romantic heart.

"Well, even if people can't come, we'll have the most important thing—an eager bridegroom," Mercedes had murmured to Megan several days later. "I've never seen Jeb so happy."

No one who was around Jeb for five minutes could doubt his passion for his new bride, but was passion alone strong enough to endure?

As Megan bent over the tie down beside her Piper and worked the damp, prickly rope loose, she felt a fresh pang of guilt. She should be at the Big House helping Mercedes with last-minute wedding details.

But Megan had gotten out of bed with an irresistible craving to get away, to be alone, if only for a little while, on her wedding day. She had wanted to fly over the MacKay homestead and think of her father, to offer one last silent prayer that he'd come home today, if he were alive.

As she loosened the second tie down, she heard the crunch of heavy tires on caliche, the final strains of a kicker tune on a car radio before the engine was shut off. Jeb slammed the door of his Cadillac and let out a low wolf whistle.

Megan got up, a smile suffusing her face with radiance.

"Morning," he drawled, the hot light in his eyes warming her.

"Hi," she whispered shyly, brushing her fingers against her thighs.

"Running away?" he murmured.

"Just for a little while."

"Not from me, I hope."

"No. From everything else."

"I know the feeling. Mother loves to make a fuss. But it'll be over soon, and we'll be alone."

"I can't wait for that."

She went to him and touched his cheek with gentle

wonderment. He drew her closer, and she closed her eyes as he brought his mouth down to hers. She felt his lips move along the soft curve of her jawline and down the warm length of her neck. She clutched him tightly until her fingers bit into his shoulders.

A long time later, he asked, "Mind if I come, too?"

"Not if you make yourself useful."

"Jackson women don't push Jackson men around like that."

"This one does." On a breathy giggle she whispered, "Just get the chock, will you?"

Within minutes they were buckled into the cockpit, and the plane was surging down the runway and into the sky. The strip, the hangar and the lush green pastures dwindled to nothing. The red roof of the Big House glinted in the morning sun. Beyond them, as far as the eye could see, stretched the endless, table-flat range of dry creek beds and mesquite brush country.

She was caught in the sheer joy of flying, in the wonderful sense of freedom. Jeb was watching her, grinning at her, and she was glad he was with her.

"I can't believe you do this for fun," he murmured.

When she turned the plane to the west and headed for the old MacKay Ranch, Jeb frowned. Beneath them and heading the same direction as the Piper, an enormous truck was roaring down the caliche road, leaving coils of white dust whirling in its wake. Megan buzzed it so she could read the large red lettering.

Jack Robards Drilling.

Megan edged forward in her seat for a closer look. "Hey, you didn't tell me there was any new oil exploration going on at the ranch. And there's another truck over there near our old place."

Jeb shifted uneasily. His features were drawn and taut, his lips pressed tightly together. "I've been trying to cut a deal with Robards on a new gas lease, but he's one tough negotiator."

She was too caught up in flying to notice when Jeb abruptly changed the subject.

A minute later the Piper zoomed over the refurbished hunting lodge that had once been the old MacKay homestead. How she had fought Jeb to try to prevent him from changing her home, but today she wasn't thinking of that battle. She was thinking of her father, of how much she missed him. A new tension settled over Megan and Jeb as they flew low over the house and the windmill, back and forth several times. They were both remembering the happier days of her childhood, as well as the sadder ones.

"I wish…" Her voice broke. Tears were misting behind her lashes.

"I know, honey," Jeb said quietly.

She felt his steadfast gaze on her anxious face. Then his fingertips grazed her cheeks as he tenderly brushed her tears from her long lashes.

In that moment she believed that there was nothing on earth Jeb wouldn't have done to make her happy.

If they were going to have a chance for that happiness, she would have to put the past behind her.

The wedding passed in a dreamlike blur. Megan was a vision with her unruly hair falling like spirals of fire upon an exquisite gown of white lace and pearls. Numb with stage fright, she clung to her darkly handsome brother as he led her with only the aid of the polished banister down the wide, swirling staircase to the hushed throng of waiting guests packed at the foot of the stairs.

An audible gasp went through the crowd when she reached them, and she felt like a queen. Brown-faced vaqueros and their wives mingled with celebrities and Texas royalty. At Megan's request, there was to be only one wedding reception.

Jeb was standing apart. Regal. Masculine. Splendid. He moved a heavily muscled leg forward and planted a polished black dress shoe on the first step by the door. Their eyes met and touched. Never had he seemed bolder or more self-confident. Her heart did a crazy somersault, and she ached for something from him she had never wanted from another man.

Jeb. She formed his name silently on her lips, and he dazzled her with a quick white smile and an irreverent wink. Her fears dissolved.

Kirk handed Megan to Jeb, and it seemed a dream as his bronzed hand closed over hers. His warmth flowed into her. A dream as she stammered her vows. A dream as Jeb continued to gaze into her eyes and speak in a voice that was deep and tender as he pledged himself to her forever.

Then it was over. Jeb lifted her veil and kissed her, his arm around her waist like a band of steel, and everyone was dancing and drinking champagne, kissing one another and toasting. The revelry went on and on, endlessly into the night, growing more boisterous as the hours grew later.

All the Jacksons were present. Nick and Amy had come with Triple. Tad, Jeb's younger brother, had flown in from Australia. Janelle and her parents were there as well, and Byrom. Megan would have preferred to avoid Byrom and Janelle, but Byrom found Megan alone and asked her to dance.

On a whirl of music he whispered boldly into her ear. "I know why you did it, but you've just made the biggest mistake of your life."

She could not meet his eyes.

"Your backgrounds are too different," he persisted.

"We both grew up on the ranch."

"You know what I mean."

"Yes…"

His arms tightened about her possessively. "Megan, I love you."

She caught the scent of bourbon on his breath.

"Don't, please." Her voice was desperate.

"If you ever need me…" he murmured thickly.

"I will always need…a friend."

He pulled her closer, his hand damp and clammy on hers. The scent of bourbon was stronger.

"I am that—and much more."

She was aware of Jeb watching them, and she felt jittery with relief when the music ended and Byrom left her.

Jeb came at once to her side. "What did he want?"

"To tell me he was still my friend."

"You're my wife now. You no longer have the time for such a friendship."

"Is that a command, your majesty?" she purred.

"Damn right," he growled. Then he kissed her.

The florid-faced oilman, Jack Robards, was at the wedding, and he seemed to gravitate to Jeb whenever Megan was not at her husband's side. Once, as Megan was stepping inside the library, she discovered them alone and overheard Jeb say, "Don't worry, I've got MacKay wrapped around my little finger."

Jack's red cheeks purpled with delight. He was swirling bourbon in his crystal glass. "I would imagine so. Clever move—your marrying her."

Megan let the door fall closed with a loud click. "Hmm?"

Both men started. There was an awkward silence as she swept into the room. Just for a moment, she had the impression she had interrupted something private, something she had not been intended to hear.

Then masks seemed to fall over their faces. Jeb rushed forward and took her hand. "Jack, have you met Megan?"

"No." There was a sardonic glitter in Robards's bold eyes as he smiled and lifted his glass toward her in a silent toast. "I haven't had that pleasure." Then he bolted his drink and with a knowing glance toward Jeb, smoothly excused himself.

Megan did not like the man. He seemed a slippery, not-to-be-trusted sort, and as she watched him go, she turned questioningly to Jeb. "What were you two talking about in here...alone?"

Jeb forced a smile and put his arm around her. "He was congratulating me on my bride."

"I thought...that perhaps there was more to it than that."

There was a moment's hesitation.

"You're imagining things, my darling," Jeb murmured.

She could not cast off her sense of uneasiness as he led her back to the reception. She was still thinking of the incident when Janelle cornered them both on the landing. They were attempting small talk with her when Jeb was called away to the phone.

"Congratulations," Janelle murmured, managing a quivering smile after he'd gone. "You look radiant. Y-you've certainly made quite a catch."

Janelle was so pale she looked ill, and Megan's heart filled with compassion.

"I really don't know what to say," Megan stammered.

"At such times, silence is the best policy."

"I—I never meant for this to happen."

"Indeed?" Janelle's brows arched. "You did catch us all by surprise. The dark horse rushing past the grandstand in sweeping triumph while the favorite was left at the gate."

"I am sorry."

"So am I. Not for myself. For Jeb. I will get over the hurt…in time. This kind of marriage so rarely works."

"He loves me."

Janelle's eyes were luminous with mute misery and a deep pitying sadness. Finally she said, "I—I hope for both your sakes you are right."

Megan felt all the terrible doubts in her heart well up to haunt her.

All too soon the wedding and the reception were over, and Megan was wrapped in Jeb's warm arms and being whisked by private jet to Santa Fe, New Mexico, for a two-week honeymoon.

In those first magical days of marriage, Megan was too overwhelmed by the new and exciting experiences of being a bride to think of anything other than Jeb. All her doubts were forgotten. It was too wonderful just to be with Jeb every hour of the days and nights, to know that he was hers, and she was his. Santa Fe with its muted colors of coral, turquoise and tan washed with golden light and purple shadows. Santa Fe with its lazy, somnolent pace, with its sense of history, with its artsy shops and boutiques was an idyllic environment for honeymooners.

Megan and Jeb would sit for hours, holding hands, talking beneath the violet shade in the park on the main plaza. Sometimes they would stroll hand in hand by the groups of black-haired Indians sitting in a row, selling their jewelry and pottery on blankets under the portal of the Palace of Governors.

Megan and Jeb would laugh over trifles—over some amusing bit of artwork, over something one of the Indians or their children said.

Never had laughter come so easily to Megan. The bitterness of years was washed away, and for hours she would forget that her father had not given her away on her wedding day, that he would never come home and share in her new happiness.

"You were meant to laugh, to be happy," Jeb murmured one evening as he caught her hand in his and held onto it. "I haven't seen you like this since you were a child."

Sometimes their conversation grew serious. Jeb began to confide in her his anxiety about the ranch's money problems. Never before had she realized the extent of the ranch's debts. Nor had she realized the complexities of managing such a massive, far-flung enterprise. He would discuss his options—the possi-

bility of cutting back on the livestock breeding pro-
grams, selling land, of pulling out of Australia, of
branching out into some new, more profitable venture.
And she would listen.

"I didn't want the ranch, the responsibility of it
all," he said once. "I would have given anything not
to have been the oldest son, not to have had to forsake
everything I ever wanted to be because someone had
to take command. Wayne groomed me for the job,
but I wanted to be a doctor. In the end, I sacrificed
everything for the ranch, for my family."

"And do you regret it?"

His lips grazed her wrist lightly. "For a while I
did." His eyes met hers. "Not anymore."

Jeb was a passionate and demanding lover; with
him Megan found that she was equally so. They made
love at any hour of the day or night in the fabulous
suite of rooms with its pink stenciled walls and adobe
balconies looking out over the desert and distant blue
mountains.

On their last afternoon in Santa Fe, Jeb and Megan
were lying quietly in bed, the sheets thrown aside,
their naked bodies entwined. Megan was trembling
faintly from their passionate lovemaking. Jeb was
stroking her hair.

"Do you realize, sleepybones," drawled his lazy
voice, "that we've been in Santa Fe for two weeks
and haven't really seen any of the sights?"

She wanted only to bask in this wanton paradise of her senses. "I don't care."

"We haven't driven into the Jemez mountains, gone to Los Alamos or seen the ski basin."

She opened her languorous eyes and tried to focus them, but Jeb remained a delicious blur of brown skin and muscle. Her hand slid lovingly across his thigh. "I don't care," she whispered, pulling him even closer, snuggling her face against his throat, taking in the scent of his clean masculine flesh, the exquisite sensation of his body against hers.

"What are we going to tell people we did for two weeks?" he muttered huskily.

She giggled. "Let them guess."

"How could we be here and not at least go out to the Puye Cliffs and the Indian ruins?"

Megan exhaled softly in amazement. "You're really serious about all this?"

"Yes."

"I couldn't drag myself to the Puye Cliffs if my life depended on it."

Tenderly he kissed the tip of her nose. Then he held her close for a moment longer, cherishing her.

Megan stayed in the hotel while Jeb went out to the Puye Cliffs. While he was gone, she ran a bathtub full of lavender-scented bubbles and sank beneath them. She had been soaking for a while when the telephone rang. She dragged herself out of her bath, wrapped herself in a towel and caught the phone.

"Howdy," came a rough Texas drawl. "Jackson around?"

"This is Mrs. Jackson."

"I guess that's close enough. Tell him his gas well came in."

"His well?"

"And it looks like his hunch was right. We've got the biggest field in years. Robards is getting set to drill a second well up by that old hunting lodge. And tell Jackson old man MacKay finally signed the lease and got it back to Robards."

"Old man MacKay…" Her voice faltered.

In that first tortuous moment of dawning horror and shock, Megan grew absolutely still.

"Y-you, you can't mean Glen MacKay is alive?" she whispered.

"Hell, yes. That ornery old coot's still kicking."

Megan clasped a second hand around the receiver to hold it steady. "You're absolutely certain he's alive?"

"Jack Robards wouldn't drill a water well without a legal lease. MacKay signed all right!"

Glen was alive!

She gazed into space. A smothering feeling enveloped her, cutting off her breath.

Her father was alive!

Jeb must have known it for ten years, and he hadn't told her! Not even on their wedding day when she'd been drowning in sorrow because she'd believed Glen dead!

Jeb had gotten her father to sign a gas lease, but he hadn't bothered to get him home for the wedding.

Jeb had driven Glen away, kept him away.

The pink adobe walls with their pink stenciled Indian drawings looked surreal, blurring and fading, then becoming so piercingly brilliant that her eyes ached in their sockets.

Jeb. Her only love. Her only enemy. His duplicity astounded her.

The vivid pinks and blues faded into a gray-tinged darkness, and her eyes misted over. A deadening coldness seeped into her, and her insides were freezing. Her extremities felt like deadweights. Her toes, her fingers, were no longer part of her.

From a long way away, she heard someone at the door shouting her name, but these sounds faded into nothingness.

The phone dropped through her fingers, and the floor rushed dizzyingly up to meet her.

Megan opened her eyes. She was in her nightgown in her bed, and Jeb was cradling her in his arms. Another man stood in the shadows. She saw the glint from the stethoscope looped casually around his neck. A syringe glimmered from the bedside table.

Jeb was talking to the doctor. "She was on the

phone when I came in, staring at me, but I don't think she could see me.''

"She's conscious."

Jeb turned and realized she was watching him with slitted eyes that were immensely cold and darkly green.

She felt the heat of his hand crushing her fingers, the burning of his mouth as he kissed them with fierce, possessive urgency.

He held her hands pressed to his cheek. "Megan, darling, you fainted. Who was that on the phone?"

She stared at him mutely.

"You're pregnant," Jeb said softly. "If only I'd known, I would never have left you."

He went on talking, but she didn't hear him.

Pregnant! She couldn't be carrying Jeb's child! Not now!

She twisted her face and buried it in her pillow.

His fingers were in her hair, smoothing it. "Honey! I know it's sooner than we would have planned, but don't turn away, not from me, not when you've just made me the happiest man in the world."

He seemed to care so desperately. Pink walls spun crazily until Megan was reeling with nausea. She kept her face buried and pressed her hands to her aching eyes. If only she could shut out his voice as easily.

"Go away, Jeb. Just go away," she whispered.

The shock of learning about her father, plus this new revelation, was too much. Pain bent against pain, twisting, suffocating, numbing. Jeb had betrayed her, and now she was tied to him forever. By the strongest tie of all, his child.

Hurt, anger, humiliation, disappointment and sudden panic combined into one total heartache that suffused her body.

She would have given anything to be alone, but Jeb was lifting her, crushing her to his body, cradling her protectively, brushing away her tears, peering into her anxious face, and she was shaking and clinging to him and despising herself for her weakness.

"Honey, you don't really want me to go. You don't mean that."

"I do! I do!"

A look of uncertainty passed between Jeb and the doctor. Then the faint hollow echo of Jeb's voice came to her as if from a great distance. "We're going home tonight, darling. I'm going to take care of you. Everything is going to be all right."

A sudden violent tremor swept through her, and she closed her eyes again. Her fingers gripped his arms like claws as he brought his lips to hers.

She shrank away in revulsion.

Nothing would ever be all right again.

A silent, unapproachable Megan allowed Jeb to see to everything, and soon they were back in Texas, alone in their bedroom in the Big House. An alarmed Jeb had explained to his parents that Megan was too tired to do anything other than retire. Thus, he had spared her the need to face her in-laws and their questions. There was an emergency meeting of the ranch's board members scheduled for the next morning, and Wayne was anxious to review several pressing items on the agenda. But Jeb put his father off and followed Megan to their bedroom.

Upstairs, Jeb put Megan to bed at once. She agreed only when he promised to sleep in another room. He gave her a dark quizzical look and decided to humor her.

When she fell asleep, her old nightmare returned to haunt her. She was a child, lost and abandoned. She called out in terror, her cries the most piteous of sounds. Jeb flung the door open and stood paralyzed listening to her sob. He knew she wouldn't want him, but he couldn't bear the sound of her unhappiness. Slowly he stepped inside and went to the bed, drawing her gently into his arms.

"Oh, Jeb," she breathed. Her arms slid around his neck desperately, clutching him in terror. Her entire body was drenched with perspiration. She was trembling, and the softness of her breasts brushed the hard wall of his chest. He fought to ignore the heat of his pulse, the hot urgent tensing in his loins.

She continued to weep. "You're going to leave me, too!"

"No," he whispered.

"I don't want to be alone again! I don't care what you've done!"

He nuzzled his roughened cheek against her soft one and pulled her closer, burying his lips in her hair, catching the scent of wild roses. "I'm here, Megan. I'll always be here."

Her fingers tightened convulsively around his neck. He couldn't understand her pain, but he could feel the intensity of her need for closeness now, the beginnings of her response to him, of his own to her.

With a pang of guilt he realized that if he were a gentleman, he wouldn't take advantage of her weakness and need for comfort, but his own need was too great. Slowly he unbuttoned her nightgown and slid it over her head, and she lay beneath him, a woman, all peach-gold skin and fire. His woman. Gloriously hot. Soft and yielding. Unprotesting. Wanting him now as he wanted him.

She was carrying his child.

He wanted to protect her from all hurt. He was overwhelmed by his tenderness for her, consumed with the need to bury himself in her, to feel the velvet walls of her lithe body close warmly around him.

Very gently, he whispered the words that once she would have given anything to hear. "I love you."

She sobbed even more frantically and twisted her head from his, wondering if he was lying about this, too. All her life she had hungered for love, but she'd been betrayed too many times by too many people to believe him now.

He touched her cheek and felt the wetness of her tears. "Tell me what's wrong."

"I-it's no use. Talking never changes anything."

He brushed her lips with his fingertips, and she opened her lips, sucking in a thick sun-browned finger. He lowered his mouth and placed a gentle kiss on her tousled red curls.

"I love you," he whispered. "That's never going to change, either."

Her shaking fingers reached up and touched him, guiding his mouth to hers with gentle urgency.

He drank deeply of her lips, of the jewellike purity of her tears, and she melted into him on a voluptuous sigh of hopeless longing.

In that moment, her need was so great that it no longer mattered that he had lied. She wanted him despite everything. Even when she had hated him, she had wanted him, and this was no different. He had betrayed her. She loved him still.

He filled the burning void of darkness with desire. Her deep, aching loneliness was held at bay by the warmth of his kisses, by the hard, seeking intimacy of his body.

Just this one last time she had to have him.

Sensing her reluctance, he took her time and again that night, wanting her to need him, wanting to reassure himself of his claim on her, wanting to know that she was really his, and discovering that she was slipping away even as he wakened her to new heights of insensate pleasure.

When it was over he fell asleep at once.

Megan lay beside him, knowing that her marriage was over. Her body felt numb and frozen in despair, her emotions imprisoned in a cell of ice.

She felt ashamed for wanting Jeb, for having turned to him for comfort after her nightmare, for the ache in her soul that craved his words of tenderness as well as the outpouring of his physical love.

Would she always be that abandoned child? So starved for love she no longer even had her defiant pride?

She was deeply ashamed. For wanting him. For loving him.

For letting him love her, this one last time.

Twelve

Megan stood in a darkened corner of Jeb's office, her bright head drooping over the lease that her father had signed less than three weeks before. Gingerly she traced a fingertip along the wavering flow of black ink that formed the letters of her father's name. Then she jerked her hand away as if burned and remained so still, so silent, it hardly seemed she breathed as she read and reread his signature with rapt absorption.

Her father was alive!

She was glad Jeb had been forced to go into town early that morning for an emergency session with the board. Glad she'd been able to convince Jeb to leave her when he'd said he didn't want to. Glad, because it had given her a chance to discover irrefutable proof that her father was alive.

There was a note attached to the document. She lifted it to the window and read her father's shaky scrawl through the blur of her tears.

> Jeb,
> Please open a special account for Megan and Kirk and place any royalties received from this venture in it, to be divided equally at some future point between them.
>
> Glen

For a long moment Megan could not tear her eyes from her father's signature. Then she crushed the thick legal-sized papers in her shaking fingers and leaned heavily against the window.

She felt like screaming, like weeping. Instead, assailed by memories, she closed her eyes. The intensity of her emotions staggered her. She'd grown up motherless, fatherless, but the most terrible thing of all, was that it hadn't had to be that way. So much happiness had been stolen from her by her father's rejection, by Jeb's silent duplicity through the years.

She dragged her eyes away from the lease. Flickering shadows floated in the eerie light. Papers and file cabinets were askew from her hours of rummaging. She had to set everything straight again before Jeb got home, but she lacked the strength.

At least she knew the bitter truth.

She sank into Jeb's chair. Her father was alive! And living in Texas. Jeb had known it, but she couldn't blame Jeb entirely for his absence. Glen hadn't wanted her!

A thousand thoughts pounded in her head, a thousand hurts. For years she had longed for her father. She remembered all the lonely birthdays, the lonely Christmases, her confusion, her stubborn proud denial, Kirk's silent grim retreat into himself every time she'd come to him in pain, her own anger and defiance. It was a galling irony that through the years the one person who had stood by her, who had guided her through the turmoil of her adolescence had been Jeb, her bitterest enemy.

She had never dreamed that Glen could callously stay away, that he would not come if he knew how much his children needed him.

He had known, and he hadn't come.

Megan forced herself to concentrate on the lease and made another equally damning discovery.

She was rich. Very, very rich. Although Jeb had won the MacKay ranch in the poker game, Glen MacKay had retained the mineral rights. One-sixth of the gas royalties were to belong to Kirk and herself.

Naive as she was about the oil business, she knew one-sixth was an immense percentage and could amount to hundreds of thousands, even millions of dollars. Megan remembered the roughneck's words. "Looks like we've got the biggest field in years."

She was soon to be a wealthy woman, and Jeb had married her, knowing of this possibility, doubtless planning for it. Numbly she flicked through the remaining sheaf of papers. There were carbons of letters Jeb had written her father through the years as well as a multitude of letters from her father. Many of them dealt with the gas exploration on the MacKay lease. But the most recent letter was a brief note from Glen thanking Jeb for saving Kirk's life.

Glen had known about Kirk, and he hadn't come.

Slowly, carefully, Megan set the documents back in their folder and filed them in the cabinet. Meticulously she went about the task of straightening Jeb's office, working with the silent, mechanical, soulless efficiency of a robot.

What a fool she had been to fall for Jeb a second time. She had been better off believing him a scoundrel.

What kind of man was her husband, anyway? He had given up his career to help his family save the ranch. He had stolen her own father's ranch, but he'd nurtured and educated his daughter. Jeb had saved her from making a disastrous marriage and hired her as his ranch pilot. Then, after all the good he'd done, when he'd realized gas lay beneath her father's lease, Jeb had married her out of greed.

She thought of the child she was expecting, and

even though she would be tied to Jeb by this baby, she felt no remorse or even regrets about it. Already she loved it.

When at last she finished straightening the office, she went outside into the hard brilliance of the day. Her senses were too vivid. The colors were over-bright. The balmy heat seemed like an oven's fire despite her cotton sundress. It was almost noon, but she felt queasy and unenthusiastic at the prospect of facing Wayne and Mercedes over lunch. Nor was she ready to confront Jeb with all that she knew when he came home.

But where could she go?

Slowly she walked toward Kirk's cottage, and when she found him gone, she remembered he was with Jeb.

She let herself inside, poured a cup of milk and made herself a cheese sandwich. But she left the meal untouched on the kitchen table, wandered into the darkly shuttered living room and sank listlessly into Kirk's favorite chair. Hours passed, but she had no awareness of them, no awareness of the sunlight turning to gold, then red, of the heat going out of the afternoon as the shadows deepened and slanted into every corner of the house. She sat in dismal, forlorn silence, her fingers tensely knotted on her lap, her mind anesthetized with pain.

She was still sitting in the dimness, lost in her world of private desolation, when she heard Byrom's

Porsche in the drive. When he strode briskly onto the porch and knocked, she got up slowly and met him at the door.

He scarcely recognized the gaunt, thin-faced woman framed in the half-light of the doorway. "Megan?"

Nervously she smoothed a tangle of hair out of her eyes and nodded.

He was shocked by the dull agony in her eyes.

She pushed the screen, and it creaked on its rusty hinge. "I was waiting for Kirk."

Byrom stepped inside. The room was musty, closed, disused. "In the dark?"

He reached for her arm, but she brushed him away, knowing instinctively that if she surrendered to his sympathy, her emotions could overpower her.

"Is something wrong?" This time he seized her by the hand and was shocked by the iciness of her flesh. "You're freezing! Are you sick?"

Blood pounded in her temples. "I'm not sick! Not like you think. Oh, Byrom…"

Carefully he folded her into his arms. "I've been worried about you."

She laid her head against his chest and said weakly, "You promised to remain my friend."

"I will always be that. What's wrong?"

For a long moment the silence of the room enveloped them.

"Everything!"

The whispered word was like a crack in a dam. All day she had wrapped her agony in silence, and suddenly it all came pouring forth.

Outside a Cadillac roared to a halt behind the Porsche.

Neither Byrom nor Megan heard the car door slam, nor the angry footsteps storming up the sidewalk. They were conscious only of the melancholy flow of one heart's anguish.

"No one has ever loved me," Megan finished on a hushed sob. "Not even Jeb."

She was still in Byrom's arms when the door crashed open and Jeb stalked inside.

Guiltily Byrom and Megan broke apart.

Jeb was like a black giant in the doorway with the flame of a dying sun behind him. His voice filled the room like thunder. "What the hell is going on here?"

"We were just talking...." Byrom began.

Megan couldn't lift her eyes to her husband's.

Jeb saw only the agony in her face. The knowledge that Megan had chosen Byrom to confide in instead of himself consumed Jeb with a blinding, raging jealousy.

"Get out, Ferguson! Now! And don't set foot on my property again."

Megan paled. For an instant, shock held her motionless. Then she lurched desperately toward the door after Byrom.

A hand gripped her arm, spinning her around.

"Not you, my love," Jeb rasped. His dark face was livid, agonized.

His hands dug into her arms. She scarcely felt the pain as he snapped her roughly against his body.

"It's not what you think," she whispered. "I came here to be alone, to wait for Kirk! So did Byrom."

"The hell you say! I told you this morning Kirk was going into town with me."

She stared at her husband in dumb amazement. "I—I forgot about Kirk going with you. Until I came here and found he was gone," she murmured. "I stayed anyway so I could be alone."

She yanked her arm free and began to run again, but he caught her effortlessly, spinning her around, bringing his face down to hers and studying her with a savage intensity. "You damn sure weren't alone when I got here."

"You're hurting me."

Brutal fingers squeezed flesh to bone. "Do you think I care? I want to hurt you. What do you think it felt like to come here and find you in this empty house all alone with the man you dated before me? Talking to him in whispers when you won't have anything to do with me? Now I see why you pleaded with me to go without you this morning."

"Will you please let me go?"

"Not until you tell me."

"You don't care!"

"The hell I don't! I've been worried sick about

you! The only time you've wanted me lately was when you woke up screaming from your nightmare. Something's wrong, and I've been waiting for you to tell me what it is! I thought you were better this morning, or I would never have left, no matter what the emergency. It's obvious you've been crying all day. Why? I want to know what you're feeling, thinking, and you're shutting me out. Is it the baby? Don't you want our baby? Megan, we have to be honest with each other...."

"Honest?" She began to tremble violently. "You don't even know the meaning of that word."

"What the hell are you talking about?"

"I'm talking about years and years of lies!" she cried. A deathlike quietness fell between the man and woman in the shadowy room. "I'm talking about my father," she said quietly.

Their gazes locked for a moment. She struggled to blink back fresh tears. His own face was as bloodless and unyielding as a granite statue.

One glance and he understood everything. He read her disillusionment and despair. He saw the end of his marriage, the end of all his dreams. His head began to throb. There was a dry cottony taste in his mouth that didn't go away even when he swallowed.

His bruising hands fell to his sides, and he looked guiltily away as though he found the enormity of her sadness unendurable, as though he knew the enormity of his own failure to tell her everything was unforgivable.

"How did you find out?" he asked at last, denying nothing, his own voice as quietly hushed as hers.

"One of Robards's roughnecks called you in Santa Fe to tell you about the gas well," she managed softly. "He told me instead."

"I see."

"I went to your office this morning. I read all your letters to my father and his letters to you. After that...I didn't know where to go, so I came here. I talked to Byrom only because he was here, and I had to talk to someone. Anyone but you."

Jeb flinched. Her cold words were like a blade of ice piercing his chest.

"I'll never, never forgive you for driving my father away!"

Something inside him broke. "That wasn't all my fault! As long as we're being honest, you played a part in driving him away yourself. You and your stubborn MacKay pride. You couldn't understand that there was no way he could hold onto his ranch. He couldn't run it at a profit, and he couldn't live with failing you. Through the years I tried to talk him into coming back, but he wouldn't listen. You MacKays are a proud and stubborn breed."

Megan stared at him, numb with shock. "That was a low, cheap shot, Jeb Jackson. Blaming me...when it was your own greed. You took his ranch. You wouldn't let him come home! And if that wasn't bad enough, when you found out there might be gas under all that land, you decided to marry me so you could get your hands on my royalties."

Her harsh words raked across his soul in a sudden, cruel, tearing pain. He stiffened proudly. His chiseled face grew as white and cold and closed as stone. "If that's what you think, then go."

There was something in his voice she'd never heard before—hurt, defeat. Something about his proud, lonely stance caught at her heart, but she swallowed, struggling to push down an inexplicable compassion for him. She clenched her hands and willed herself to continue. "You've never done anything that wasn't motivated out of greed or the lust for power, Jeb. I tried to delude myself into believing I was wrong about you. All I'll ever want from you now is a divorce."

"No!"

"You said I could go..."

"You're pregnant with my child! No divorce."

For a paralyzed second, they stared into each other's eyes. Then she leapt past him and ran into the darkening twilight of the late afternoon.

She heard the crashing of his boots behind her, but she reached his car first and saw his keys dangling in the ignition. She hopped inside, snapped the automatic door locks and headed for the hangar and her airplane.

* * *

Megan was in her Piper, and Jeb was shouting to her from the runway.

She ignored him and started the engine. The propeller became a faltering, blurred arc. There was the smell of exhaust.

A storm of sound erupted into thunder, drowning out Jeb's cries.

She was overwrought. She shouldn't go up when her emotions were in such chaos.

But she was too upset to think rationally.

All she knew was that she had to get away from Jeb and be alone. Everything would be all right if only she could get away.

There was only the single runway, and that afternoon there was a crosswind.

Megan raced down the strip, anyway.

Just as she lifted off, the wind caught the tail and the plane was thrown back against concrete, nose first. The tip of the propeller scraped but kept whirling, and the plane bounced up into the air again. The Piper turned crazily into the wind. With a damaged prop, Megan knew her only chance was to try to land.

She fought to get control of the plane, but the Piper slammed onto the runway at a crazy angle. A wheel broke and crumpled beneath the fuselage. A wing tip ground suddenly down onto concrete, spraying sparks as the plane careened toward the hangar. Megan's head crashed violently into the instruments.

Megan's world was pain and terror and the acrid smell of burning rubber. Plumes of black smoke engulfed the plane. Spirals of flame shot everywhere.

She pounded against the door, but it was locked. The cockpit was like a furnace. She fumbled with the catch to the door, and it came undone. But she was pinned into her seat. In the distance she saw Jeb's face, wild and dark with fear as he tore down the runway in a breakneck run.

He would never reach her in time.

She was going to be burned alive.

The last thing she thought of was their baby.

Thirteen

Vaguely Megan sensed the poisonously sweet odor of antiseptic enveloping her like a cocoon of death. For days she drifted in and out of consciousness with pain stabbing her like the sharpest and hottest of knives. She had broken two ribs, her collarbone, fractured her skull and suffered a concussion. Sometimes when she slept, she was haunted by her old nightmare. Sometimes by a new one—that her baby was dead and she herself was dying. She would awaken screaming in her cold, glassed-in cell. She wanted Jeb then, but he was never there. An intensive-care nurse would come and whisper soothing, meaningless niceties and give her a shot.

Megan no longer cared what Jeb had done, how he might have betrayed her. Pain and terror had obliterated everything but her need for him. She longed for the strength of his arms holding her, for the deep melody of his voice caressing her, comforting her, but now he didn't want her.

Dark days blended into dark nights, and he never came. Because he didn't, she knew the most profound sense of loss and abandonment she had ever known. Her mother's leaving was as nothing. So was her father's. Only Jeb mattered. He was her heart. Her soul. Life itself. She had accused him. Judged him. Without giving him a chance to defend himself.

Her last memory of him was of his dark haggard face through the flames, his rage washed away by hideous fear, his strong hands untwisting metal, his arms closing around her, pulling her from the fire, his hoarse voice shouting for Lauro.

Jeb had carried her to the house. He had held her in the ambulance. She remembered his black head pressed against her side, the silent heart-wrenching agony of his tears. He had lifted his grief-ravaged face, seeking her forgiveness, and she had only stared at him with dull, hopeless eyes and forgiven him nothing.

She'd been stubborn and defiant.

Now it was too late.

From a deep sleep Megan came awake into a shining world filled with familiar faces. Mercedes and

Wayne were there talking to each other in hushed, worried murmurs.

A single ray of sunlight streamed into the room and lit a tangled crop of cotton-white hair. The man's head was bowed, his gnarled, sunburned hands clasped tightly together, but she knew him instantly.

"Daddy!" Her voice floated away, dying, the thinnest fragment of sound.

But he heard her.

She shut her eyes, thinking it all a dream, but when she opened them again, her father's craggy, seamed face, darker and more leathery than she remembered, was bent anxiously to hers.

"Girl?"

She reached up and tried to touch him, but her hand fell away.

Kirk stood beside their father. Mercedes and Wayne were behind them. Megan scanned the room, seeking Jeb, but he wasn't there.

"So, you've decided to wake up and hold court at last?" Glen said gruffly.

"Oh, Daddy." She tried to reach her hand up again, but it fell back limply to the bed. "It's really you?"

"The prodigal father," he said in a low gravelly tone filled with shame. "Can you ever forgive me?"

Her anger toward him was gone.

"Just love me," she whispered, "and don't go away."

He bent over her. She wanted to hug him, to shower him with kisses, but she was too weak to do anything other than smile when he traced her cheek with his fingertip.

"I never was so scared in all my life, girl."

"Neither was I. My baby?"

"The baby's fine."

She sighed weakly. Glen's voice faded. His image blurred. She struggled to hold onto it, but it was lost in a mist.

Her baby was alive! Her father had come home!

There was only Jeb who was lost to her.

Glen was still there when she woke up again. This time he was seated beside her, and her hand was folded tightly in his work-worn palm. "Girl, I thought about you everywhere I went."

"Why'd you go? Was it something I..."

"Hush. None of that kind of talk. Darlin', of course it wasn't your fault. It was only 'cause I was losing the ranch, and I couldn't face you. I was bankrupt, and Jeb gave me enough money for a new start. Only I didn't do so good with that, either, so I couldn't come for you like I'd planned. Jeb promised me, no matter what happened, he'd take care of you."

"You shouldn't have left me. I was so mixed up. For years I was so mixed up."

"I see that now. Money isn't near so important as other things."

"I blamed Jeb, Daddy, for everything. I thought he took the ranch out of greed."

"It's true he'd always wanted our land, but he tried to talk me out of gambling the ranch away. The way I saw it, it was better to lose it fair and square in a card game, than sell it for nothing. I reckoned everybody would hold it was just the MacKay wildness cropping up again. Besides, I told Jeb you'd never forgive me if I sold. I knew you'd be mad at him for winning it, but I reckoned he could stand your hate better than I, 'cause I loved you more than he did. Only I was wrong, 'cause he loved you more than I ever did. I was no good for you, Megan, not like Jeb's been. He was father, brother, husband. He loves you in all the ways a man can love a woman. I was weak. Your mother saw it. She left because I failed her. I couldn't face failing you, too.

"Through the years, Jeb's begged me to come home. He wanted me to come to the wedding. He came to me and threatened to kill me almost, but I was too stubborn. Don't be so hard on him for not telling you, 'cause he was caught between the two of us. I thought you were better off without me, that I'd only hold you back. I wouldn't've come now except Jeb didn't give me a choice. He said you might die if I didn't, and he wasn't going to let you die without me coming home. Can you forgive a foolish, weak man?''

"Oh, Dad... We MacKays can be such fools." Her voice softened. "You no more than I. I...I was so wrong about Jeb. I thought he only married me because of that gas field."

"Hell, girl, that's utter hogwash. It was 'cause of him we got that royalty! It was only 'cause of him negotiating that we got the one-sixth royalty instead of the usual one-eighth. He wanted that for you 'cause he knew how bad you'd always felt about losing the ranch. He wanted you to have something that was yours so you'd feel like you were more his equal. Only he couldn't tell you about any of it 'cause I made him promise not to. I didn't want you knowing about the mineral rights until they amounted to something you could be proud of. Honey, I won't say he's perfect. He's a Jackson, and they're a grabby, stubborn bunch of rascals. But he loves you. He climbed into that burning plane and got you out only seconds before it exploded. He broke his hand getting you out of there. He could have died. Till you woke up, he was here night and day. Then he went home. 'Cause he said you didn't want him.''

"But I do want him!"

"Then I guess you'll have to swallow your MacKay pride—I know it's a mouthful, but do it anyway. Here..." Glen picked up the phone and briskly dialed Jeb's number. Then he handed the receiver to her. "Tell him how you feel, girl. Now."

Glen walked out the door just as Jeb answered.

"Hello."

The masculine salutation was deep and low and melodious. It jarred every nerve ending in Megan's body. Queasy with a sudden fear, her mouth too dry to speak, all she managed was a low, strangled garble.

"Hello?" Jeb repeated, a faint edge of exasperation lacing his voice this time.

Desperately she swallowed. "J-Jeb…it's just me… just your wife." Her voice died away.

"Just my wife." He repeated her phrase, only somehow it came out twisted and bitter. "Megan?" His voice hardened when he said her name.

"Yes."

He said nothing more for a while, but the hollow silence between them was charged with raw emotion. Her heart began to pound violently as she tried to fathom what he was feeling.

"It's good to hear from you," he said at last in a formal tone she'd never heard him use before.

Her stomach knotted.

"I've been keeping up with how you've been doing," he said.

"But you haven't come by?"

"No. You made it pretty clear how you felt."

"I…"

"I've decided that I'll do whatever you want. Divorce."

She wanted to cry out that she loved him, that she missed him, that she was sorry for everything. In a tiny choked voice, she whispered, "B-but I—I don't want a divorce. Not now. The baby…"

"Then a legal separation. Whatever. You can go or stay. It doesn't matter anymore, Megan. I swear I'll agree to anything you want. The important thing is for you to get well, for you to take care of yourself and the baby."

She bowed her head, cupping the receiver tightly against her ear. Scalding tears slipped from her eyes. There was nothing more to be said.

Very slowly she hung up the phone. She didn't even realize he was still talking.

Her marriage was over. Jeb couldn't forgive her for what she'd done. Not that she blamed him. He had never been anything but gallant and heroic. He had been her dearest friend, her mentor, her lover. He had always taken care of her, always loved her. How had she repaid him? With hatred and distrust.

She began to sob in earnest. Nothing mattered but Jeb, and he was lost to her forever.

With a hopeless sigh of exhaustion Megan sank onto the double bed in their bedroom and watched Jeb. He moved with tense, jerky motions, as if he felt as awkward and ill at ease as she did. She knew he was deliberately keeping his back turned toward her while he heaved her suitcases on the luggage racks, snapped the locks and opened them.

Jeb hadn't visited her once in the hospital! Not once. Not until today when he'd shown up with his parents to bring her home. She'd been stunned when she'd glanced up and seen him in her doorway, his darkly handsome face grave and uncertain. Then he'd crossed the room and pecked her perfunctorily on the cheek. At the brisk touch of his lips, her breath had caught in her throat and a violent quiver had darted through her stomach. Since that moment he'd scarcely looked at her, scarcely spoken to her.

Now that he was alone with her he was even quieter than he'd been in front of his parents. How he must hate her for all she'd done!

Jeb turned. His tanned face was paler than usual. There was a forbidding, hard line to his mouth. For a fraction of a second their eyes touched, and she attempted a shaky smile. But he didn't bother to return it, and she looked away quickly.

"I moved my things into the room next door," he said grimly, his voice harsh and loud as if it were an effort to even speak to her. "I'll be going now if there's nothing more you need."

Megan got up carefully and moved toward him. He stopped, his gaze slanting indifferently to her vulnerable face. An embarrassed flush warmed her cheeks.

His own features were hard and set, his black eyes dark and unreadable.

"Jeb..."

She had to try to talk to him again. It didn't matter that her heart was pounding with fright. It didn't matter that she would have to humble herself and beg his forgiveness. If only he would listen.

"Don't go," she whispered desperately. "Please. Not yet. Stay a little while longer."

"What for?"

Slowly she came to him. As she did her gown fell off her shoulder. Jeb tensed as he stood in the middle of the room, watching her, his gaze transfixed.

She went to the dresser and lifted the statue Glen had carved. Her pale fingers caressed the smooth wood.

"Do you remember the day," she whispered, "Daddy carved this?"

Jeb closed his eyes and took a deep breath. "You know I do."

"I loved you then," she murmured. She came closer and tilted her head back, so that her hair spilled down her back like plumes of flame.

She seemed lost, fragile, dazzling. Never had he wanted her to love him more. He steeled himself. "You were a child," he ground out. "You didn't know your own mind. You can keep the statue, if that's what you're after. I'm sorry I took it. It doesn't mean anything to me any longer. Nothing matters...any longer." He tried to look away from her, but he lacked the strength of will.

She let her gown fall lower, down her arm, and his black gaze was mesmerized by the soft curve of her throat, by the soft pale golden shoulder.

She bit her thumbnail and glanced up at him through the thickness of her downcast lashes. "But I'm not a child now. I know my own mind now," she murmured. The fire in his eyes made her heart skip a beat. Self-consciously she let her fingers trace the length of the male statue lovingly. "And you're wrong about the statue not meaning anything."

"Get to the point," he muttered in a tight voice.

She tossed the statue onto the bed, went to him and took his bandaged hand in hers. He towered over her like a frozen and unyielding giant. She thought he wanted nothing so much as to escape the pain of her presence. She didn't know how the mere sight of her aroused passion and other emotions he was determined to kill. Her gentle touch set him on fire.

She clutched his cold fingers more tightly. "Oh, Jeb, I know you want to go. You can't bear the sight of me, but I can't let you until I tell you how sorry I am. For everything. I was so wrong. So stupid. So blindly selfish, so careless of your feelings. I can't blame you for hating me now."

He started, his eyes burned into her. "What are you saying?" His voice was unsteady.

She could feel his hand trembling.

"I love you," she moaned softly. "I love you. I always have, and I always will. It was wrong of me to blame you for what happened to my family, wrong of me not to understand you would never steal our ranch, wrong of me not to recognize all that you did to try to help me. Kirk tried to tell me, but I wouldn't listen. It was too easy to blame you. Oh, Jeb, I want you to be my husband. I want our baby." She raised his injured hand to her lips and kissed his fingers, one by one. "More than anything."

He watched her, saw the imploring sadness in her face, saw her love for him shining in her upturned face, and at last the guarded look left his eyes. Gently he wrapped his arms around her and kissed her on the mouth, a long, tender, undemanding kiss.

"I wanted to tell you about your father. So many times," Jeb murmured. "But there's no talking you MacKays out of things, no convincing your father he was wrong."

"I know."

"And I didn't marry you for money. There's no telling whether there'll be all that much of it, anyway, Megan. You're part of everything I am. Of everything I've ever been. We love the ranch, the same things. Our children, half-MacKay, half-Jackson, will grow up here as we did, loving these same things. Whatever I took from you, I give back to you as my wife. I'll sign the MacKay acres over to you and Kirk tomorrow if that will make you happy. All that matters to me is your happiness. I need you to help me if we're going to hold onto the ranch for our children. Darling, you're my wife. Everything I own is yours.''

''Everything I own is yours, too.'' She held onto him as though he were life itself. Gently she touched his bandaged hand, kissed it. ''You were hurt... because of me.''

''Don't you understand? I would have died—to save you.''

She gazed into his eyes, and some terrible restraint inside her broke. She was loved. Truly loved. At last, by the one person who had always stood by her through the darkest hours of her life, by the one person who had never left her. Never again would she be a lonely little girl crying herself to sleep in the dark. She would have Jeb.

''Forever,'' he whispered. ''You will belong to me forever.''

This time she gave him no argument as he slowly led her to the bed and pulled her down beside him.

''I'm going to reform you,'' she said. ''No more cigarettes and no more coffee.''

He chuckled. ''I'd better corrupt you in self-defense,'' he murmured.

Gently, without speaking, he drew her into his arms. His lips touched hers, and Megan felt her soul rising up to meet his. For a long time there were no sounds other than the exchange of soft kisses and loving caresses and gently whispered promises between them.

Marriage. It meant family, love, children. The threshold of a new life forged together. All the things she had spent a lifetime longing for were hers.

* * * * *

A LETTER FROM THE AUTHOR

Dear Reader,

This story will always be special to me, not only for its characters, Megan and Jeb, and its south Texas setting, which are very real to me, but because certain events in my own life inspired me.

When I was growing up, we had several airplanes and lots of adventures. Both my parents were pilots. My father was very cerebral about his flying, but my mother was far more emotional. And as a result, she had more adventures. Over the desk in her office hangs the bent propeller from their first plane, with the inscription Close Encounter. One day when she was practicing her short-field landings, she came in nose down, and the tip of her propeller hit the runway before her landing gear. Fortunately, she had the presence of mind to go ahead, let the plane crash, and land. If she had tried to take off again, as many pilots have in the past after such a mistake, she would not have survived. She cried for a week after that misadventure. But she got in another airplane five minutes after that wreck and went up again.

Pilots are a special breed.

And so is Megan MacKay. This book is about her and the tough man she couldn't stop herself from loving.

Enjoy!

Ann Major

SILHOUETTE Romance™

Escape to a place where a kiss is still a kiss...
Feel the breathless connection...
Fall in love as though it were
the very first time...
Experience the power of love!

Come to where favorite authors—such as
Diana Palmer, Stella Bagwell,
Marie Ferrarella and many more—
deliver heart-warming romance and genuine
emotion, time after time after time....

Silhouette Romance—
stories straight from the heart!

Silhouette®
Where love comes alive™

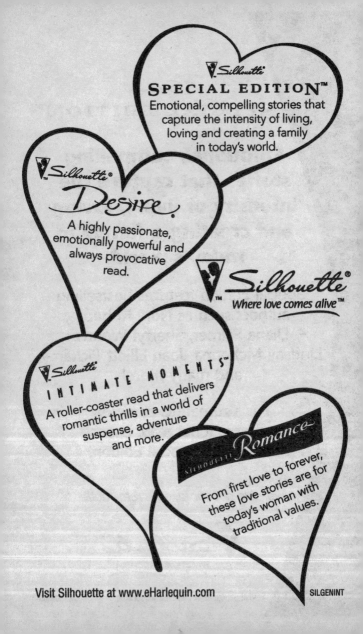

Where love comes alive™

From first love to forever, these love stories are
for today's woman with traditional values.

A highly passionate, emotionally powerful
and always provocative read.

Silhouette®

SPECIAL EDITION™

Emotional, compelling stories that capture the
intensity of living, loving and creating a family in
today's world.

Silhouette®

INTIMATE MOMENTS™

A roller-coaster read that delivers romantic thrills
in a world of suspense, adventure and more.

Visit Silhouette at www.eHarlequin.com